Your Friend in Fashion, Abby Shapiro

Amy Axelrod

Holiday House / New York

For Mark

HOLIDAY HOUSE is registered in the U. S. Patent and Trademark Office.
Printed and bound in April 2011 at Maple Vail, York, PA, USA.
www.holidayhouse.com
First Edition
1 3 5 7 9 10 8 6 4 2

Library of Congress Cataloging-in-Publication Data

Axelrod, Amy.
Your friend in fashion, Abby Shapiro / by Amy Axelrod. — 1st ed.
p. cm.
Summary: Beginning in 1959, Abby, nearly eleven, writes a series of letters
to Jackie Kennedy, each with sketches of outfits she has designed, as she
faces family problems, concerns about neighbors, and her own desperate
desire for both her first bra and a Barbie doll.
ISBN 978-0-8234-2340-8 (hardcover)
[1. Family life—Massachusetts—Fiction. 2. Adolescence—Fiction.
3. Fashion design—Fiction. 4. Neighborhoods—Fiction. 5. Jews—
Massachusetts—Fiction. 6. Letters—Fiction. 7. Onassis, Jacqueline
Kennedy, 1929-1994—Fiction. 8. Massachusetts—History—
20th century—Fiction.] I. Title.
PZ7.A96155You 2011
[Fic]—dc22
2010024185

Contents

Then one morning she wasn't paying attention while crossing the street and walked into the path of a horse-drawn peddler's cart. Her right big toe was crushed when the wagon wheel ran over her foot. Now she's got this huge bunion and wears a size 8 D shoe on the right foot and a size 7 B on the left. So she's a little unbalanced when she walks. Anyway, I know there's a lot more to the story, but Auntie Rina won't share every last detail.

"What's the point?" she says. "Talking about a smashed foot reminds me of smashed dreams. Who needs to stir up the pot of bad memories?"

I know I'm a lucky girl to have so many dolls. Most of them are foreign dolls that customers in our store brought to me from their travels. So far, I have thirty in my collection. I also have some regular store-bought dolls, like a Heidi doll with a music box inside, a baby doll that tinkles after you feed her a bottle of water, a dancing doll with straps that attach to my feet, and a ballerina doll. Auntie Rina gave her to me after my first ballet recital. Her costume is a pink tutu, just like the one that I wore.

The only doll I want but don't have yet is a Barbie™ doll. Susie Applegate already has a Barbie. She got it just this past March when the doll was brand new in the toy stores. Her father bought it for her and it wasn't even her birthday. She says that her father buys presents for her and her mother all the time just because he loves them. Susie says every day is Valentine's Day in her house. Susie lies about a lot of things, but not about this. I've been in her house and seen her father in action. One time Mr. Applegate came home early from work with flowers for Mrs. Applegate and a box of chocolate-covered cherries for Susie. Then, right then and there, he grabbed Mrs. Applegate around the waist and twirled her about the kitchen. He dipped her backward with one of those fancy dance moves you see in a movie musical, just like a regular Fred Astaire. And when he lifted her up, he smooched her on the lips. I have never, ever seen anyone kiss somebody on the mouth

like that in public. That's certainly not something my parents would ever do.

I've been interested in fashion design
since third grade, way before the Barbie doll
even existed. That's when I started making
paper doll fashion models with lots of changes
of outfits. Auntie Rina bought me some sketch-
books to encourage my talent. She says an
interest in fashion runs in our blood. My family
not only owns a very fancy women's shoe store,
but Auntie Rina has subscriptions to fashion
magazines like *Vogue* and *Harper's Bazaar.* She
says it's very important for her to know what's
in style. That way she can stock the store with all
the right handbags and accessories to match the
shoes. Auntie Rina runs the front of the store
with Mummy's help. Uncle Morris runs the back
and is the shoe buyer. My father, Hank, is one of
the shoe salesmen. Uncle Morris gave him a job
when he and Mummy got married.

Third-
Grade Paper
Doll Fash-
ion Model

When Mummy and I were out shopping
last week looking for back-to-school clothes, I
dragged her into the toy store so she could get
an up close look at Barbie.

"Oh my God!" my mother shrieked loud
enough to wake the dead. "That doll has big bosoms!"

"So what," I said. "You have bosoms. Auntie Rina has bosoms.
It's perfectly normal for a woman to have bosoms."

"But dolls are toys," she said. "Toys aren't supposed to have
bosoms. I find that highly peculiar."

So then I figured this was my big opportunity to ask Mummy
for a bra. I told her that my best friend, Anna Maria Tucci, wears
a training bra.

"Mrs. Tucci said she couldn't have Anna Maria walking around jiggling the way she was," I said. "In case you haven't noticed, I jiggle, too."

No comment from my mother.

"So when can we go to Mayfair's, the undergarments store? That's where Anna Maria got her bra."

"You want a brassiere?" Mummy said a little too loudly for my tastes. "First it's a Barbie doll and now it's a brassiere?"

"Oh, Mum, go announce it to the rest of the world, why don't ya?" I said. "And while you're at it, please try not to be so old-fashioned. Call it a bra, not a brassiere."

"Abby, you're not a woman yet. You're only turning eleven," she said. "You're going into sixth grade. You're still a little girl and little girls don't need bras."

"But I do need a bra. Age has nothing to do with it. Trust me. I've got these little mounds already. I'll show you when we get home."

"It's not necessary to show me, because I can see as plain as day that you don't need a bra. You're as flat as an ironing board. End of discussion."

That's how it always is with Mummy. When she doesn't want to talk about something, it's "end of discussion."

"But what about a Barbie doll? Can I get one for my birthday?" I asked.

"Abby, *hak mir nisht ken tshaynik*!"

Mummy said in Yiddish that she wants me to "stop knocking on her teapot," or, in other words, stop driving her nuts. Yiddish is the language that Jewish people spoke in the old days in Europe, and I know a lot of words because my family still speaks it at home.

"You're getting your bedroom redecorated for your birthday," Mummy said. "That's a very expensive gift, and it's from the whole family. So don't go asking Auntie Rina to buy you the doll, because you know she will. She spoils you enough as it is."

I don't even bring up the possibility of getting the doll for Hanukkah. My family never gives toys for Hanukkah. My brother and I get money to put in our savings accounts or stuff that we need, like clothes or books.

"That means I'll have to wait until when?" I asked. "My birthday next year? When I'm in seventh grade?"

I could hear Susie Applegate's stupid rule about giving up dolls ringing in my ears.

"I think you should come up with a plan to earn the money. It's important to understand that money doesn't grow on trees," Mummy said.

"Fine."

Actually I don't mind earning the money. It might be fun. I'll just have to come up with a really good plan. And when I get my Barbie doll, I'll play with her for as long as I want. And if Susie Applegate ever calls me a baby, I'll march her over to our store and Auntie Rina will set her straight once and for all. That's what I'll do. Maybe. And then again, maybe I won't. Susie Applegate is a *yenta* and a *nudnik*. In Yiddish that means she's a "nosy busy-body" and an "annoying pest." Maybe instead I'll just give her a plain, old-fashioned knuckle sandwich smack in the kisser. That'll take care of her big mouth real good.

2

Bunny Bunny Bunny Bunny Bunny . . . Rabbit

"Come on," my brother, Marty, shouts at Todd Silver. "Batter up already!"

Tonight we are not playing the Whiffles against the Ponytails. The boys' team is called the Whiffles because they all have whiffle haircuts, not because we are playing wiffle ball. When you get a whiffle cut, the barber buzzes your hair right off. It's so short that when you run your hand over it back and forth real fast, it feels soft and fuzzy, like a brand-new pair of flannel pajamas before they've been washed. The only part of the haircut that isn't short is the bangs. The boys use something called a whiffle stick to make those bangs stand up tall and straight like a picket fence. The stuff comes in a tube and reminds me of arts and crafts paste. It works really well, which is a good thing because if those boy bangs fell down on the forehead, the haircut would look stupid and girly.

The girls' team is the Ponytails. There are three of us on the team, but I'm the only one who actually has a ponytail. Anna Maria Tucci has a pixie, and Janine Lipson has a pageboy. But they're both letting their hair grow, so as soon as they can pull it back with a rubber band, the team name will make more sense.

Marty is captain for the month of August. When you're captain, you can change the rules if you feel like it. For example, when Todd was captain for July, he decided that we should play wiffle ball more like a game of baseball.

"No more ghosties. Set up better bases," he ordered, "because we're going to run and outfield for real."

So Todd rounds up all these neighborhood kids to make our teams bigger. I like it much better when we have ghost runners. It's more fun to hit, make it to first base, leave your ghost runner there, then return to home plate to be up at bat again. If you get another hit, you run back to first and your ghostie goes to second. Me and my ghostie, who I named Veronica, always make it back to home plate. The only reason Todd made those changes is because he's a show-off. Marty says he always comes in first at school in the fifty-yard dash. It was also a very stupid rule change. During the month of July the Whiffles and the Ponytails lost almost all of our wiffle balls. Maybe Todd can run bases fast, but he can't play outfield worth a hill of beans. He never uses two hands to catch a sinker, and he can't throw back a grounder in the right direction. That's how come all of the wiffle balls ended up where they're not supposed to be. Plus the fact that the new kids on the team are only going into second and third grade. It's because of all their fumbles that we're down to our last ball. So tonight might very well end up being our last game for the season.

Now that it's Marty's turn to change the rules, he decides to fire the new kids, go back to running ghosties, and mix up the team players. He picks me because I am the best pitcher. I can outpitch Todd Silver and Harry Degen any day. I could outpitch them both blindfolded. My fastball, curveball, knuckleball, and death grip pitches make the Whiffles jealous. My best friend, Anna Maria Tucci, is on the team with me and Marty. Janine Lipson, who is going into seventh grade, is playing with Todd and Harry.

Todd keeps digging his feet in, only they're not going anywhere. We're playing on the paved road, not in some sandlot.

When he's not squirming and wiggling around, he adjusts his grip on the plastic bat and swings these fake little practice swings.

"Let's go, Todd," I yell. "Batter up before my birthday next month!"

"Shut up, Abby," he yells back. "I'll batter up when I'm good and ready!"

Todd doesn't like me much. That's okay. The feeling is mutual. When Mummy was the Cub Scout den mother, I always wanted to be included in whatever Marty and the boys were doing. Todd tripped me one time on purpose, so I bit his leg. I sunk it in real good and broke some skin. Mummy was mortified and offered to pay for his tetanus shot.

The Whiffles and the Ponytails have been playing ball on our street, Darlene Avenue, for two seasons. I looked up the definitions of both "street" and "avenue" in my junior dictionary, and I can't see that there's much of a difference in meaning. Both words are defined as roadways or thoroughfares. The man who used to own all the land named our avenue after his daughter, Darlene. I guess it's really something special to have an avenue named in your honor, but Darlene doesn't live on Darlene Avenue, so I can't see where the fun in that is. Darlene Avenue is great for playing wiffle ball, dodgeball, or red rover because there's very little traffic.

"Two-minute break," Todd yells. He drops the wiffle bat and runs like crazy up our driveway. He's going into our house to use the bathroom. When Todd gets nervous, he pees a lot.

While we wait for Todd, I check out the neighborhood. I see the television lights flicker through Mrs. Lazarus's living room picture window. Her house is a square, brick house, the smallest on Darlene Avenue. It reminds me of the third pig's house in *The Three Little Pigs*.

Mrs. Lazarus is very old. Her eyesight is so bad that she can't read anymore. She likes the television and leaves it on all day. She says it keeps her company and doesn't sass back the way family members do. I can't comment about her family members, because I've never met them, but I, myself, have been guilty of sassing many times. Mrs. Lazarus also loves chocolate because her husband used to own a candy factory. Sometimes she leaves candy bars for us on her front steps even when it's not Halloween. But she never does it during July and August, when they could melt all over the place and attract every ant in Massachusetts.

Next door to Mrs. Lazarus's house is a cute little bungalow. It's the kind of house you might see in the movies, where a glamorous star might live. Just picture Doris Day in a sundress and a big hat picking flowers and singing, "*Que sera, sera,* whatever will be, will be." But Doris Day doesn't live in the bungalow. The neighbor who lives there is a nice enough woman but, to quote Mummy, is a *farshtunkene shikker,* which means a "stinking drunk."

I think I know the difference between a regular drunk and a stinking drunk. My father drinks every night before supper and then some more after supper until he falls asleep in the green easy chair in the den. I guess that makes him a regular drunk. But Mrs. Whelan guzzles booze like water all day long and does really crazy things when she's on a bender. One time she went outside in the middle of the night and began parading up and down the street singing, "Here she comes, Miss America," at the top of her lungs, waking up the whole neighborhood. She wouldn't let anybody put her to bed until we pretended to present her with a crown.

I hear her voice calling me. "Yoo-hoo, Abby."

Mrs. Whelan is taking out her trash. I've never peeked inside her trash can, but Mummy says that there's nothing in there but empty liquor bottles. I don't know how Mummy knows this unless she's snooped in there herself.

"The woman eats like a bird. That's what true alcoholics do, you know," Mummy says. "They drink instead of eat. Come to think of it, I don't believe I have ever, not even one time, seen Gladys in the grocery store."

My mother tends to exaggerate sometimes, but I have to agree with her that Mrs. Whelan is pretty skinny. Her legs look like toothpicks sticking out of her Bermuda shorts. I guess that's another difference between a regular drunk and a stinking drunk. My father always has a big appetite and cleans his plate.

The Ponytails and the Whiffles, minus Todd, who is still in the bathroom, wave to Mrs. Whelan. I keep a tight grip on the wiffle ball and run over to say hello. Mrs. Whelan gives me a big hug while I help her wheel out the trash can.

"Abby, I haven't seen you in the longest while," she says. "What grade are you going into this year?"

"Sixth grade," I tell her.

"My, my, how time flies," she says. "I remember when your parents brought you home from the hospital. It seems like yesterday. You were so cute with that pink ribbon in your hair."

"Ribbon?"

"You looked absolutely adorable," she says, and then quickly adds, "and you still are! Mr. Whelan, God rest his soul, even took a picture of you with his brand-new Polaroid™ camera. I bought a pink frame for the picture and gave it to your mother as a gift for the nursery."

Suddenly Mrs. Whelan gets quiet. Her lower lip trembles a bit.

"Are you all right?" I ask.

She touches my arm. "Oh yes, honey, I'm fine. I just get sad whenever I think about Mr. Whelan. I'll see you later," she says abruptly, and turns to walk up the driveway.

If Marty were standing next to me, I would have elbowed him and said, "Betcha she goes inside and pours herself a double cock-tail right now."

Mr. Whelan was a policeman who was killed in the line of duty. It was during a bank robbery, I think. Mummy said that was when all the drinking started, after he was killed. And maybe she's sad too because she never had any babies. All I know is that this is the first time I've ever heard anything about any baby picture of me with a pink ribbon in a pink frame.

Next door to Mrs. Whelan lives Mr. Lane, in a Cape Cod house. Mr. Lane owns cranberry bogs on Cape Cod, so it's kind of funny that he lives in a Cape Cod house, too. I wonder if he planned it that way on purpose. At Thanksgiving time he gives everyone in the neighborhood a big bag of fresh cranberries. Raw cranberries might look like candy, but you should never just pop one in your mouth. I did that once and spit it out halfway across the kitchen. Without being cooked in tons of sugar, they taste really disgusting.

Mr. Lane always looks spiffy. He slicks his hair back and wears a pressed shirt and slacks when he mows the lawn. He has a push lawn mower that does not have an attached bag to collect the clippings. He just leaves them there as mulch on the lawn. Mummy says he "cuts a fine figure and would be a good catch for some young lady." But Mr. Lane lives with his mother, so I guess nobody's caught him yet.

My father has come outside to do some yard work before it gets dark. He's always doing battle with the Japanese beetles. They eat up our rosebushes, which climb the picket fence in front of our house. I think he spends half his life pruning, fertilizing, and spraying them, and still the beetles win.

Two seconds later my mother comes out to report that Todd will be out shortly.

"Oh, for God's sake, Hank," she says, "can't you change your clothes? It's embarrassing for the whole world to see you dressed like that."

My father wears a ratty, stained T-shirt that used to be white and ripped seersucker pants. And he's got a cigar butt hanging out of his mouth. He never lights it; he just chomps on it. My father takes the cigar out of his mouth and spits on the ground.

"Take a hike, Betty," he says to her. "But before you do, take a good hard look at yourself in the mirror. Where do you get the gall to criticize me?"

The heels of my mother's slippers angrily clop, clop, clop up the driveway. The hem of her housecoat has come undone in the back. It's flapping against the backs of her legs. I look away.

The five-year-old twins who live next door see my father and run over to the fence.

"Uncle Hank, Uncle Hank," the girls say, "whatcha got for us today?"

"Close your eyes and hold out your hands," my father says.

He reaches into his pants pocket for a brand-new box of Chiclets™. He shakes the box first, like he's doing some kind of magic trick, then fills their palms with little candy-coated squares of gum. The twins open their eyes and squeal with delight. There's never any offered to the Whiffles or the Ponytails.

I hear the toot of a horn as a car comes down Darlene Avenue. The driver pulls over in front of my house and sticks her blond, beehived head out the passenger's side window. It's Mrs. Riordan, the divorced lady who lives around the corner. Mummy doesn't approve of her. Besides the fact that one of her kids had nits really bad and infected Marty's whole first-grade class, Mummy says she's a flirt, a floozy, and a man-eater, and any woman with a drop of sense in her head should never let her husband within two feet of Mrs. Riordan, otherwise she'll steal him away.

My father comes in close and leans his arms on the car door. I listen while they *shmooze*, make stupid small talk about the muggy weather and how she's so thrilled for taking his advice and buying the pair of metallic silver sandals with the ankle straps, and not the pair with the toe thongs. My father nods in agreement. "I told you so," he says. Then she says, "Oh, Hank, you are by far the best shoe salesman in the entire world. I wouldn't buy my shoes from anybody but you."

"Oh, Blanche, stop," he says, waving his hand in fake protest.

I close my eyes for a second and wish Mrs. Riordan would steal my father. Maybe Mummy's watching from the living room window and is wishing for the same thing, too. Before I open my eyes, I squeeze extratight for good measure.

Anna Maria walks over to me as Mrs. Riordan drives away. "She's some flimsy, that Mrs. Riordan," she says.

"It's 'floozy,' not 'flimsy,'" I tell her.

"Didn't Mrs. Riordan have to have an operation on her shoulders because she wore her bra straps too tight?" Anna Maria asks.

"Yup," I answer. "One and the same."

While Anna Maria goes over to talk to Janine, I look past Mr. Lane's house and see the big white Victorian with the wraparound porch. The shades on the windows are dark green and are usually pulled low. The house is set way back from the street, so we can't see inside the house but we know who lives there. My Auntie Rina calls them *machsheyfes,* which in Yiddish means "witches." The two sisters look like real witches in their long-sleeved black dresses with black scarves on their heads. They dress like that even in the summer when it's sweltering hot and your clothes get stuck in every crack of your body and you have to tug to free them up when you think nobody's looking.

The witches are outside every day of the year sweeping their porch or driveway. They don't have shovels, so they use their brooms instead to remove the snow in the winter. And when they are done sweeping, they sit in their rocking chairs on the porch and stare at all the kids who pass by on the street or on the sidewalk. Sometimes they shout things in witch language that are probably curses or swear words.

Todd finally comes running down our driveway. He takes his place in front of the chalk X on the street, which is home plate.

"What took, Todd?" I ask. "Number one turn into number two?"

The Whiffles and the Ponytails like my joke and burst out laughing.

Todd turns purple in the face and chokes the bat like he's trying to kill it. He's probably imagining that it's me.

"Shut up and pitch," he says.

Todd gives me a fierce look, so I decide to send him my best-ever lefty curveball. I wind up and let it fly. Todd whacks the ball, and to everyone's surprise it sails high through the air—past Mrs. Whelan's house, past Mr. Lane's house, and onto the witches' lawn.

"Nice goin', Todd, you doofus," Harry Degen yells out to him. "I guess season's officially over now."

The wiffle ball is right smack on the middle of the lawn, but because the lawn is big and sloped, it is slowly rolling downward toward the street. The witches lean forward in their rocking chairs. First they eye the ball, and then they eye the Whiffles and the Ponytails.

"Go get it, Abby," Todd says. "It's your fault. You pitched it."

"Yeah, you think you're so tough all the time," Harry says. "Get the ball."

I look at Marty. He doesn't say a thing. He just shrugs his shoulders and lifts his eyebrows at the same time.

"Go ahead, Abby, I dare you," Todd says.

"Fine, I'll get it," I say. "You're all a bunch of sissy scaredy-cats, anyway."

"Wait, Abby," Anna Maria says, grabbing my arm. "Do the bunny. It'll protect you."

"I thought that only worked for ghosts and zombies in cemeteries," I say.

"No, I'm pretty sure it works for witches, too," Anna Maria says.

I suck in as much air as my lungs can hold. Then I run faster than that showoff Todd Silver can any day and repeat "bunny bunny bunny" over and over again as I slowly let out air, reach the ball, grab it, and run back to the chalk X. I drop the wiffle ball and say "Rabbit!" with my last gasp of air.

The kids go home as the fireflies come out. That's the parents' rule. Marty and I walk up our driveway. He holds the bat and I hold our precious wiffle ball.

"Nice move there," Marty says. "That showed guts."

"Thanks."

Marty opens the porch door. We hear them arguing through the kitchen window.

"Hank, you've had enough," Mummy says.

"Shut up with your two cents, Betty," he says. "Just for that crack I'll have another."

We wait quietly on the porch until they both leave the kitchen. This bickering is nothing new. I should be used to it after all this time, but it still gives me a bellyache. And lately they've been fighting worse than ever.

"I don't know why they got married," Marty finally says. "Or why they stay married."

I nod. I really don't know anything about how my parents met, except that they got married "late in life." That's a direct quote from Mummy.

The plain truth is that I can't name anything about my father that I like. Not even one tiny thing. Not even if somebody gave me an Indian sunburn for hours or pinned my arm behind my back so high up that it felt like it would snap off like a dried-out wing from a roasted chicken. I just couldn't do it. And the way I feel, Marty feels a lot worse. He calls our father the Invisible Man. But I think he's more like Dr. Jekyl and Mr. Hyde. To the neighbors and the customers at the store, he's nice Dr. Jekyl. But to the family at home, he's mean Mr. Hyde.

"You know how Mummy gets all wound up," Marty says. "Maybe they won't get a divorce, because Mummy will worry if we come from a broken home, we'll turn into a pair of JDs."

"Ha! Fat chance of that! There are so many adults in this house, we'd never turn into juvenile delinquents. Not with the way everyone hovers over us," I say.

3

If It's Tuesday, It Must Be Lamb Chops

"So, Abby, tell us about your first day of school," Auntie Rina says at the dinner table.

"It stunk to high heaven," I tell her. "This is the first time I am not in the same class with Anna Maria. She's got Mr. Polonski and I've got Miss Burns."

"Yes, that is a shame," Auntie Rina agrees. "You girls have been together every year since kindergarten."

"But here's the worst part of sixth grade so far," I say. "Susie Applegate is in my class. And she sits at the desk right next to mine. Sitting next to her from nine till three is worse torture than listening to somebody drag their fingernails on the blackboard."

"Excuse me, Abby, I hate to interrupt, but could you please pass the piccalilli," Uncle Morris says.

"That's almost a tongue twister," I say.

"Yowzah," Uncle Morris says.

I don't even know what the word "yowzah" means, but it's one of Uncle Morris's favorite words.

I make a scrunched-up face as I reach in front of my plate for the bowl of wet green whateveritis. It looks like seaweed or slime that came from *Twenty Thousand Leagues Under the Sea*.

"Yuck," I say as Uncle Morris takes the bowl of piccalilli from me.

Uncle Morris sits to my left at one of the long sides of the upstairs dining room table. This is where we eat dinner every night. The downstairs dining room is saved for best, like a very special occasion. But we almost never eat there, because we rarely have any special occasions.

"I'll have another lamb chop," Marty says.

"Finish what's on your plate first," Auntie Rina tells him. "Then you can have seconds."

Marty is going on fourteen. He's had his Bar Mitzvah, which is supposed to mean he is a man. But Auntie Rina talks to him like he's a little boy.

My father points to the platter of lamb chops to have it passed down his way. His seat is to my right at one of the heads of the dining room table. My father never talks to any of us during dinner. He just eats in silence with his head hung down, not making eye contact. Marty thinks he looks like a cow who is chewing its cud over and over and over again.

"You're always so dramatic, Abby," Mummy says. "I think the only reason why you've taken a dislike to Susie Applegate is because she has a Barbie doll and you don't."

I roll my eyes at Mummy.

"No way, Jose, that's not it at all," I say.

"I saw that face," Mummy says. "Keep it up and your eyes will get frozen in that position forever, and then you'll have a face that not even a mother will love."

"Very funny," I say. "Hardee har har."

Marty kicks me under the table and motions with his head toward Uncle Morris. We watch him ladle out big globs of the piccalilli relish and pour it all over his lamb chops. It's Tuesday, so it's lamb-chop night.

Mummy does all of the cooking for the family and she follows a strict schedule. There is a set menu and it never, ever changes, unless, of course, if it's a Thanksgiving Thursday, when we'd normally have meat loaf but instead have turkey and stuffing. Or if it's a Jewish holiday, then Auntie Rina makes chicken soup with her famous giant *matzoh* balls or stuffed cabbage. Otherwise it goes like this—

SUNDAY: Roast beef, baked potato, salad, and cherry
  Jell-O™ with fruit cocktail.

MONDAY: Fish, baked potato, salad, and orange Jell-O
  with pear halves.

TUESDAY: Lamb chops, baked potato, salad, and lime
  Jell-O with peach halves.

WEDNESDAY: Tomato soup, grilled cheese sandwiches,
  potato chips, and strawberry Jell-O with pineapple.

THURSDAY: Meat loaf, baked potato, salad, and lemon
  Jell-O with grapes.

FRIDAY: Roasted chicken, french fries, salad, and baked
  apple.

SATURDAY: Franks and beans (Marty's favorite) and
  black cherry Jell-O (my favorite).

Mummy gets nervous when things don't go according to plan. She gets flustered and forgets things. That's why she likes to have everyone sitting in their assigned seat at six o'clock sharp. It's a real hoot to go to the supermarket with Mummy when she does the weekly shopping. She always says out loud when she grabs a wagon, "Now, what shall I buy this week?" like it's something she really has to think hard about. "Mum," I always say, "you could grocery shop blindfolded." Then she gets angry with me and says I shouldn't criticize her. "I do the best I can," she says. My mother has no sense of humor.

"So if it's not because of the doll, then why don't you like Susie Applegate?" Auntie Rina asks. "I'd really like to know."

"I couldn't possibly count the reasons. Susie Applegate is a drip and a pill. She's a drippy pill. Let's just leave it at that."

There's no way I'll tell Mummy or Auntie Rina the truth about why I hate Susie Applegate. It would hurt their feelings. What happened with Susie Applegate was that I invited her over one afternoon last year at the beginning of fifth grade. It was the first time she'd ever been in my house, and it was the last. She wore out her welcome on the first shot.

"Your house is so big," Susie said the second she walked inside. "You must be rich."

I didn't know if we were rich or not. Susie insisted on getting the grand tour, so I showed her the kitchen, living room, dining room, den, bathroom, my parents' bedroom, and my bedroom.

"Where's your brother's bedroom?" she asked.

"Upstairs," I told her.

"You mean he has the whole upstairs all to himself? This I gotta see!"

Before I could stop Miss Know-it-All Susie Applegate, she was already up the back staircase.

"This is so freaky," she said. "Your brother has a room in somebody else's house? I didn't know you lived in an apartment building, because it sure doesn't look like an apartment building from the outside. And why does everything upstairs look just like everything downstairs? Do you have copycat neighbors? I mean the furniture and the rugs and the drapes and everything is the same. Oh, and the wallpaper, too. I left that one out."

"This isn't an apartment house," I said. "It's one big house with two floors that's big enough for my whole family."

"You got more brothers and sisters?" Susie asked.

"No!"

This girl was so exasperating.

"My family includes my two uncles and my aunt," I said.

"What! Your aunt has two husbands?" she asked. "That's against the law!"

Susie Applegate should learn to keep her mouth shut because with that comment she crossed the line from nosy idiot to stupid idiot.

"Of course not. What an incredibly immature thing to say."

I said that to sound so much smarter than her, which I am, anyway.

"My Auntie Rina is not married and neither are my uncles Morris and Max. They are my mother's sister and her two brothers."

Susie Applegate had an odd look on her face, like that information didn't quite register. Her skull was as thick as set concrete that even a jackhammer couldn't bust open. Susie Applegate was giving me a royal headache. I began to understand why when I don't stop talking, Mummy has to take two extrastrength aspirin and lie down in her dark bedroom.

"Well, how come they aren't married?" she asked.

"I don't know. They just aren't," I answered.

"Everybody in the whole world grows up and gets married," she said.

"Well, I guess not everybody. So you're wrong on that one."

"I want to see your uncles' bedroom," Susie said, and without asking, pushed past me to the first of the two closed doors.

She burst out laughing when she saw the twin beds with matching red-and-blue-striped sheets and bedspreads.

"My four-year-old cousin has the same sheets on his bed."

"That's it! Tour's over! Downstairs," I ordered.

"But I didn't see your aunt's bedroom," Susie said.

"Tough noogies."

I gave Susie a push in between the shoulder blades to get her going down the staircase. I would have liked to have pushed much harder. She stopped short at the last step and turned around to face me. She was way too close for comfort.

"I bet when you grow up, you'll live with your brother, Marty."

"No I won't. That's a stupid thing to say. If I get married some-day, I'll live with my own family," I told her.

"But your mother doesn't. Why don't you and Marty and your father live in your own house, like normal people? My mother says that all little girls grow up wanting to be exactly like their mothers, so you're gonna be just like yours."

"My mother's a nice person," I said. "Be careful what you say about her."

"I'm sure your mother is nice and all, but she sure looks old. Gee, for your sake I hope she doesn't go and die on you soon. My mother just turned thirty-four. What's your mother's age?"

I didn't answer Susie's question. My mother, Betty, is in her fifties. I'm not stupid. I know that's old to have a young kid. But I never really cared about that. Mummy has always told me and Marty that she loves us and that we mean the world to her. I know that's the truth, and that's all that counts. Mummy never lies.

"It would be a shame if you ended up like your mother. I mean, heavens to Betsy, she looks like a hobo. That sweater she's wear-ing has a hole in the elbow. Mother would never wear anything that shabby, even to do housework. And your mother is missing a tooth. Hobos have missing teeth. That's all I'm saying."

I burned from the top of my head to the soles of my feet. I was angry, but I was also ashamed. I knew it was true what Susie said about my mother and I hated her guts for saying it. And maybe I hated my mother some, too, for letting herself go and being all sloppy. She wears that torn sweater to work and her stockings usually have a run up the back. I'm embarrassed to be seen with her at home and out in public, especially after she had that tooth pulled. It's been over a year and she hasn't gone back to the dentist to have a fake one made. I bugged her about it for a while, until she got all upset and yelled at me. "I'm well aware of it, Abby," she said. "I'll go to the dentist when I'm good and ready." Then she said, *"genug!,"* which is Yiddish for "enough," or "end of discussion!"

Marty kicks me again under the dining room table. He sits opposite Uncle Morris and in between Mummy and Auntie Rina, who sits at the other head of the table. Marty refuses to sit next to our father. Marty's pointing to the piccalilli with his right index finger and pinching his nostrils shut with his left thumb and forefinger. He mouths "disgusting." Really, Marty's one to talk. He pours ketchup all over everything he eats. It's the worst at breakfast, when he drowns his scrambled eggs till they look like squished squirrel guts. Half the time he's not even paying attention to what he's doing, because his nose is buried in an issue of *Popular Mechanics.*

"Uncle Morris, could you pass that piccalilli back to me?" Marty asks.

"Sure thing," Uncle Morris says excitedly. "I didn't know you liked piccalilli."

"You bet!" Marty says.

Uncle Morris is beaming. Uncle Morris and Uncle Max try to be positive role models for Marty, since my father doesn't count for much in the parent department. Uncle Morris helps him with scout projects or with anything that involves hammer and nails or dangerous tools like an electric saw. Marty plays the saxophone in the junior high school band, so he needs all of his fingers.

Uncle Max tries in his own way, but Auntie Rina usually gets angry with him for his efforts. She says he's a little *meshugga,* which in Yiddish means a little "crazy." Like the time right before Marty's Bar Mitzvah. Uncle Max told Auntie Rina that he'd be delighted to take Marty to Hebrew school and give him advice about the importance of becoming a Bar Mitzvah and carrying on our Jewish traditions. But instead he took him to the racetrack. He let Marty sip his whiskey, puff his cigar, and bet on greyhound dogs. Marty had the time of his life. I was pretty impressed when Marty said he didn't turn green from the cigar or throw up from the whiskey. Uncle Max's explanation to the family was that because Marty was almost a man, there was no time like the present to start celebrating.

But Uncle Max isn't around much, so he doesn't get a chance to corrupt Marty very often. He's usually at his nightclub downtown playing poker with his buddies. We keep his dining room chair up against a wall, and if he shows up to eat with us, he squeezes in between my mother and my father.

Auntie Rina is always mumbling something about Uncle Max carousing with some new dame. She disapproves of all of his girlfriends, so Uncle Max never brings them around. Auntie Rina called his new girlfriend, Dolores, a *shiksa*. I told her, "So what if she isn't Jewish! She sounds nice and Uncle Max really likes her."

"Oh yeah, Uncle Morris, I love pick-a-lil-lee," Marty says.

He overpronounces every syllable, but Uncle Morris doesn't get it.

Marty spoons just a drop onto his plate and, when nobody is looking, dabs his finger into it, then sticks his finger into both of his nostrils. Then he blows piccalilli snot rockets across the table, which hit me in the chin. I don't care. Anything Marty does is a-okay by me. He quickly wipes his nose with his napkin. That's always how it works in this family. He never gets yelled at. Nobody ever sees any of Marty's shenanigans. If I just pulled what Marty did, I'd probably shoot the piccalilli all over Mummy and be in deep trouble for days.

"Oh, Mummy, before I forget, Miss Burns wants us to bring in baby pictures of ourselves. She wants to make a bulletin board with them and this year's school pictures," I say.

"Okay, I'll see what I can find from the photograph album."

"Where's the one with me brand-new from the hospital with a pink ribbon in my hair?" I ask.

Auntie Rina and Mummy look at each other.

"What photo are you talking about?" Mummy asks.

"The one Mrs. Whelan said her husband took with his Polaroid camera. The one she put in a pink frame. She told me all about it."

Mummy clears her throat. "Such a photograph doesn't exist," she says.

"Gladys Whelan has a good heart. But she has problems, Abby. You know that," Auntie Rina says. "You can't believe everything that comes out of her mouth."

"I'd like to hear what else you have to say about Susie Applegate," Mummy says, changing the subject. "She seemed like a perfectly nice young lady when she came here after school last year."

"You know, Abby, your mother is right. It's really important to always look for the good in people and give them a second chance if they've offended you in some way," Auntie Rina says. "Especially this time of year."

The Jewish High Holy Days are coming up next week. Rosh Hashanah and Yom Kippur are the holidays when we're supposed to think about our actions over the past year and repent for anything we've done that was wrong. It's kind of like a grape-juice spill on the kitchen counter. If you leave it there, it gets all sticky and little fruit flies show up. But if you wipe it down really well with a clean wet sponge, then the mess is gone and you get to start over fresh. That is, until the next grape-juice spill.

"I think it is not very important to talk about Susie Applegate. What is important is that Anna Maria is not in my class for the first time in my history at Alexander Graham Bell Grammar School. I think you should go to Principal O'Leary's office immediately and file a formal complaint about the matter."

Suddenly there is a loud noise at the table. My father slams his silverware down and a dinner plate with the pattern of the landing of the Mayflower breaks in two. Lamb chops stain the white tablecloth. He bolts up, and his chair teeter-totters back and forth for a few seconds before it steadies. Five pair of eyes watch him storm out of the dining room like a two-year-old throwing a tantrum. Nobody says a word. I said the whole thing about filing a formal complaint with the principal as a joke, since everybody knows you don't go to the principal to *kvetch* about putting your kid with her best friend in the same class. I honestly wasn't talking about the whole mess with Marty last year.

When Marty was in seventh grade, he was fooling around in homeroom with Harry Degen, and they didn't stop, even when their teacher, Mr. Forsberg, told them to settle down. The next thing you know, Mr. Forsberg lost it and went berserk. He grabbed Marty by the collar and shook him back and forth like he was trying to snap his neck. Then he stopped just as suddenly and blubbered and begged Marty not to say anything to anyone because he could lose his job.

Even if Marty wasn't going to tell, twenty other kids saw Mr. Forsberg hurt Marty, and they all went home and told their parents. By the time Mummy came home from working in the store, she already knew what happened. The news had spread that fast. She demanded that my father go to the junior high school the next morning and file a formal complaint or have the police go to the school and have the teacher arrested. She said that's what any loving and responsible father would do.

But my father said, "What's the big deal? Marty just got what was coming to him."

Mummy called him a coward and a spineless jellyfish and

said he was a poor excuse for a parent. "The issue isn't that Marty wasn't behaving. It's that nobody, and I mean nobody, has the right to touch my child," Mummy said.

So my Uncle Max and his sidekick, Sy, went to the school and took care of business. Knowing them, they probably threatened Mr. Forsberg to within an inch of his life. Just looking at Sy can scare you. He's not ugly or anything, it's just that he's a big man with black hair all over his knuckles. Marty says that Sy was a gangster and went up the river to bunk at the Big House for a couple of years. But that's all ancient history. Uncle Max was, and maybe still is, a gangster, too, only he never got caught. Anyway, the two of them gave this Mr. Forsberg a good talking-to because he didn't say as much as boo to Marty for the rest of the school year.

It is Auntie Rina who finally breaks the silence at the dinner table.

"Anyone for more lamb chops?" she asks.

4

That Miss Burns Is No Clotheshorse

I didn't have a birthday party when I turned eleven, because, as Mummy reminds me on a daily basis, redecorating my bedroom from soup to nuts was like having eleven years' worth of birthday gifts all at once. Mummy took me to the paint store in August, before school started, and told me to take my time selecting a wallpaper pattern. I looked through book after book and nothing was exactly right—until we came to almost the last page in the last book in the pile.

"Oh, I don't know about this," Mummy said. "It's a little loud."

"I love it. And besides, you promised me I could select absolutely, positively anything I wanted even if you hated it," I reminded her. "You gave me your word."

Mummy sighed and told the salesman the measurements for my bedroom. A week later the wallpaper arrived. Then the painter pasted hot-pink daisies on four walls and painted the ceiling and trim hot pink to match. It would have been even more perfect with hot-pink curtains, but Mummy put her foot down.

"You're trying my patience, Abby," she said. "Let's hang white café curtains, if you don't mind."

Actually, I did mind. I caved on the curtains, but not on the hot-pink shag area rugs.

Since Anna Maria Tucci is my best friend, she is the first to experience the magnificence of the Pink Palace, which is the new name for my bedroom. Anna Maria's birthday present to me is a pair of pink fuzzy slippers to match my color scheme. I wear the slippers while I lie on top of my pink bedspread, even though it's September hot and my feet are sweaty. Anna Maria kicks off her shoes, then lies on top of the other pink bedspread on the guest bed.

"Oh, Abby, your bedroom is so cool," she says. "You are one lucky stiff."

"I'd be an even luckier stiff if I had a Barbie doll to play with in the Pink Palace. But Mummy says I have to figure out a way to earn the money. I don't get allowance. I'm expected to do stuff around the house without being rewarded."

"Me too. I don't get paid for chores, either," Anna Maria says. "Have you seen how many girls in sixth grade got Barbies in just the few weeks since school started?"

"I know," I say. "It's spreading faster than last year's chicken pox epidemic. And what's worse is that Susie Applegate formed a Barbie club and made herself the president."

"Yuh," Anna Maria says. "They meet and switch going to one another's houses and trade doll clothes."

"It's sickening how Susie brags about having the most doll clothes. Besides the black-and-white-striped bathing suit that the doll comes with, Susie has a picnic outfit with clamdiggers, a Southern belle outfit like Scarlett O'Hara wore in *Gone With the Wind*, a dress with apples all over it, and a negligee with slippers."

"What's a negligee?" Anna Maria asks.

"It's some kind of a slinky nightgown. Kids don't wear them."

"Oh," Anna Maria says.

"Every single morning Susie leans over toward my desk and goes 'tick, tick, tick' and says the countdown to seventh grade has started. Then she laughs with that annoying horse laugh of hers and those big front teeth and says that by the time I get my Barbie, it'll be too late."

"Stupid Susie Applegate and her stupid rules," Anna Maria says. "My nonni agrees with your Auntie Rina. She says you can play with dolls even if you're an old lady in a rocking chair with three-inch whiskers on your chin."

We lie quietly on my twin beds for a few minutes until Anna Maria says, "Abby, there's something I've got to tell you, but please promise me first you won't get mad."

"Don't worry, I won't get mad. Just spill."

"My nonni says that she'll buy me a Barbie if I get a good first report card," Anna Maria says.

"Congratulations. It's in the bag. You always get all As."

"Are you mad?" Anna Maria asks.

"Nah," I say. "I'm not mad, but I am a little jealous. No, I'm a lot jealous. First you get a bra, and now you'll have a Barbie in two months. Which one are you going to get? A blonde or a brunette?"

"A brunette," Anna Maria says.

"That makes sense, since your hair is brown."

"How much money do you have saved up?" Anna Maria asks.

"Not much. A buck forty."

"Maybe you could earn money by doing stuff for people in the neighborhood," Anna Maria suggests. "Like take the trash out for the drunk lady or read the newspaper for the old woman across the street."

"I do that stuff already. And besides, in Sunday school Rabbi Levine says it's important to do good things for other people without expecting anything in return. He says when we do good deeds, we help to repair all that's wrong with the world."

Barbie Paper Dolls

"Yuh, we learn the same thing in religion class. Father Joe says we have to help our fellow man and all that jazz."

"Let's play paper dolls. I've already designed some new Barbie clothes," I say.

We sit on the pink shag rug near my desk. I hand a pair of safety scissors to Anna Maria, but instead of cutting, she twirls her bangs. She does that when she's thinking.

"Wait a minute," she says. "I've got a great idea! Oh, Abby, this is so good and it's a way to earn money."

"Shoot," I say.

"You want to be a fashion designer when you grow up, right? So why not start now? You could sell your designs for doll clothes. My nonni would be a customer. She already told me that she's going to be making doll clothes for my Barbie rather than throw the money away on those overpriced toy store outfits," Anna Maria says. "Ooooh, here's one even better! Sell the designs for grown-up clothes. Lots of ladies make their own clothes or have a dressmaker sew them."

I am excited. This is the best idea ever to come out of Anna Maria's mouth.

"Anna Maria Tucci," I say, "in addition to being my best friend, you are my smartest friend. That's exactly what I'm going to do. I'm going professional. Maybe I could even find one rich, fashionable lady who'll buy all my designs at once, and then I can get my Barbie right away. I'll have to come up with a catchy name for my design business, though."

"What about Abigail's Fashions?" Anna Maria suggests.

"No. It has to sound classier. Abigail's Fashions sounds like a discount department store to me," I say.

"You're right. That's not a special enough name."

We finish cutting out our dolls and start on the clothes.

"Make sure you don't cut off the tabs," I remind Anna Maria. "I'm out of tape, so I can't do any repairs."

"Okay."

"Oh, speaking of tape, you should have seen Miss Burns's face the other day when Mr. Polonski returned the tape dispenser he borrowed from our classroom. All he said to her was 'good morning' and 'thank you' and she blushed all the way down to her collarbone."

"She's really got the hots for him something awful," Anna Maria says.

"Don't I know! She stayed bright red all the way through attendance, the Pledge of Allegiance, and two stanzas of 'My Country 'Tis of Thee,'" I say.

I lean my head over to one side and give it a smack.

"Oh, I can't believe I forgot to show you this," I say. "I gave Miss Burns a makeover."

I take out my sketchbook from the desk drawer and flip to the back of the book.

"I made a bunch of drawings. First I drew Miss Burns in her everyday normal," I say.

"Yup, that's Miss Burns all right," Anna Maria agrees. "Her clothes are the worst."

"I'll say. That Miss Burns is no clotheshorse. She needs some oomph, some pizzazz, some zip-a-dee-doo-dah! Those nylon stockings she wears with the heavy seams up the back! Yikes! Doesn't she know that ladies haven't worn stockings like that since World War II? I know that and I wasn't even born then. And those shoes! We'd never sell anything like them in our store. Even my Auntie Rina with her miserable feet wouldn't be caught dead in something so unfashionable. They look like nurses' shoes with squeaky rubber soles, only in mud-brown instead of white."

I flip the page to show Anna Maria two new, improved drawings of Miss Burns.

"Wow! She looks so young and pretty in regular clothes." Anna Maria says.

"Too bad Miss Burns can't see Miss Burns all dolled up," I say. "Maybe then Mr. Polonski would fall instantly and insanely in love with her."

Auntie Rina says that true love is when two people are meant to be together out of all the people in the whole universe. She calls it *bashert*. It means "it's fated." I once asked her why it wasn't fated for her to have a true love, and she said, "Me? I never had the time for all of that."

"What's on the back of the last page?" Anna Maria asks.

"It's the last sketch of Miss Burns. I call it my masterpiece. *Voilà!*"

"Ooh la la," Anna Maria says.

Sometimes we enjoy speaking French words to each other.

"I present to you Miss Burns as a sexpot!" I say.

"What's a sexpot?" Anna Maria asks.

I shake my head at Anna Maria. Sometimes I have to teach her everything about grownup stuff.

"A sexpot is somebody who wears their clothes hip-hugging tight. Like Mrs. Riordan. She's definitely a sexpot."

"I bet she wears one of those negligees, too," Anna Maria says.

"Definitely!"

"But Miss Burns isn't like Mrs. Riordan. She can't even say hello to Mr. Polonski without getting all embarrassed. All you did was stick her in a glamorous dress and made her look like a high fashion model. Miss Burns is a nice sexpot," Anna Maria says. "I'm sure you can be a nice sexpot without being like Mrs. Riordan, the flimsy."

"That's 'floozy,' not 'flimsy,'" I remind her.

"Close enough," Anna Maria says.

We play paper dolls until Anna Maria has to go home to set the table for supper—one of the chores she has to do for free. Before she leaves, she lets me try on her training bra. Anna Maria is very impressed that I fill it out perfectly, without a bit of space to spare.

"What are you gonna do?" she asks.

"I'll give Mummy one more chance," I say.

"Just ask your Auntie Rina to get a bra for you," Anna Maria says.

"I can't," I say.

I know that in Mummy's book, asking for a bra and asking for a Barbie doll are one and the same. If Mummy told me not to bug Auntie Rina for a Barbie, she'll flip her wig if I ask Auntie Rina to buy me a bra. She always complains that Auntie Rina undermines her authority as it is.

"You've got a problem," Anna Maria says, "especially at the rate you're developing. No offense intended."

"No offense taken. I can't go through all of sixth grade wearing an undershirt. That'll be the pits. I feel like my chest is turning into one of those wiggly bowls of Jell-O that Mummy serves for dessert every night."

"Oh, that's not good," Anna Maria says. "I hate to ask, but does Susie Applegate wear a bra?"

"Yuh. I can see the straps underneath her slip," I say.

"Sorry. That's double bad for you. Besides not having a Barbie, it won't be long before she's making fun of you for not wearing a bra, too."

Anna Maria is so right. They say bad things come in threes. I do not have a Barbie doll, I am broke, and Mummy is as stubborn as a mule stuck in quicksand. I know if I can sell my designs, I'll earn enough to buy a Barbie. I'm confident about that. It's the waiting part that's going to be hard. And as far as the bra thing goes, even if I filled out a full A cup, Mummy still wouldn't buy me a bra. Period! End of discussion!!

I have problems. Oh, yes I do.

5

The Lightbulb of Good Ideas

I open Auntie Rina's bedroom door and peek inside. Sunday mornings are our special time together before breakfast. We usually discuss fashion.

"Knock, knock. Anybody home?"

Auntie Rina is snoring. The lamp on her night table is on and there are magazines spread out all over the bed. She's even wearing her glasses. Auntie Rina owns three identical pairs of eyeglasses with rhinestones in the frames, which sparkle like real diamonds. When they get dirty or cloudy from hair spray, she cleans them with a toothbrush dipped in a solution of ammonia and water. Then she shakes them out and says, "Look, Abby, the fire is back!"

If my bedroom is the Pink Palace, then Auntie Rina's bedroom is the Lavender Palace. She's got pale lavender flowers on her wallpaper with matching sheets and bedspreads. The extra bed belonged to my grandmother, *Bubbie* Lena. She used to live with us, too, until she fell and broke her hip and had to go to a nursing home.

I place my design sketchbook on the night table. I carefully lift the bed covers and crawl underneath. Then I snuggle up like a baby kangaroo into the curve of Auntie Rina's belly. She feels warm as toast. And her bed smells so good, like her lavender soap

and hand cream. She wakes up and gives me a kiss on my head.
I flip around and return the kiss.

"Surprise!" I say.

Auntie Rina points to the bedroom next door.

"Shh, keep your voice down. The boys are still sleeping."

Auntie Rina still calls my uncles Max and Morris "the boys"
even though they are both in their late fifties. My Uncle Max
might even be sixty. I'm surprised that he slept home last night.
Lately he's been staying at his girlfriend Dolores's apartment.

"Have you been asleep like this all night?" I ask.

"Good gracious, no. I was wide awake at four in the morning
and started to read some magazine articles about Senator Kennedy and his wife, Jackie. I guess I dozed off."

"Obviously!"

"Wise guy," Auntie Rina says, tickling my ribs.

"Show me what you were looking at," I say.

I lay my head on Auntie Rina's shoulder as she opens up
Life magazine. In one of the photographs Jackie is wearing a
black-and-white houndstooth-checked suit.

"I think she looks like a movie star, don't you?"

"And how!" Auntie Rina says. "Boy, would I love to take a peek
inside her closet!"

Then she lays down the magazine and says, "Just imagine, if
Senator Kennedy decides to run for president and gets elected,
then he'll be the youngest president in the history of the United
States of America."

"Everybody in school thinks it would be neat if Senator Kennedy ran for president. You know, because he's from Massachusetts like us," I say.

"An election is important business," Auntie Rina says. "Just
because you are too young to vote right now doesn't mean you are
too young to understand what it's all about."

Auntie Rina is very patriotic. She came to America when she

was seven years old and couldn't speak a word of English. She was born in Vilna, Lithuania, which she calls the "Old Country." Sometimes she says *feh* in the same breath when she mentions Lithuania. That means in Yiddish that she doesn't have a very high opinion of it. I don't know exactly where Lithuania is on the map, but it sounds like it was a terrible place.

One time Auntie Rina had to hide in a cold barrel filled with brining pickles because men broke into their house. They threatened to kill them and all the other Jewish families in her neighborhood if they didn't give up their gold wedding bands or something else of value. She said that these attacks were called pogroms and that peasants and soldiers in the czar's army carried them out just because they hated the Jews. It all happened a very long time ago. That's why the family came to America, which Auntie Rina says is the greatest place on earth.

Auntie Rina and I continue to look through the magazine pages that have photographs of Jackie Kennedy.

"If Senator Kennedy decides to run for president, then Jackie will be thrown into the spotlight even more than she is now," Auntie Rina says. "Every woman in America will want to copy what she wears and look just like her. Whoever becomes her favorite fashion designer will have a dream career."

The lightbulb of good ideas begins to flicker in my head. I sit up straight.

"What exactly do you mean?" I ask.

"Well, there isn't a fashion designer alive who wouldn't want to design clothes for someone as important as Jackie. If Senator Kennedy runs for president, she'll first need campaign clothes, and if he wins the election, then she'll need inaugural gowns."

"How does someone get to be Mrs. Kennedy's fashion designer?"

"Well, I'd imagine designers submit their portfolio of sketches. And if Mrs. Kennedy likes what she sees, they'd take it from there and set up some kind of a business arrangement," Auntie Rina says. "I've heard that some hopeful fashion designers have already built custom-made mannequins of Mrs. Kennedy's dress size."

"Hmmm," I say.

The lightbulb of good ideas is now burning bright. I see my future so clearly. I, Abigail Leah Shapiro, will become the personal fashion designer for Mrs. Jacqueline Lee Bouvier Kennedy, Possible Future First Lady of the United States of America. Not only will I become famous, but I will earn enough money to buy a Barbie and a bra at the same time. I kick off the covers and climb out of Auntie Rina's bed.

"Gotta go," I say as I grab my sketchbook and tuck it under my arm.

"What's the rush?" she asks. "You didn't even show me your newest sketches."

"Later. I'll show you later. I have to do something."

I run down the front staircase and into the Pink Palace, where the name for my business comes to me like cold air blasting from a freezer door left wide open—Abilea Coutures. I'm not exactly sure what the word "coutures" means, except that I know it's French and has to do with fashion. I really like the sound of it...Abilea Coutures. It sounds classy, just like Jackie!

6

Dear Possible Future First Lady of the United States of America

I know exactly what I want to say to her. But putting it all down in words isn't as easy as I thought it would be. If only I had her telephone number. Then I could just call her up. I never have any problem talking to people face-to-face. I can talk forever. Anna Maria says I can make conversation about anything, even something like dust. So after three practice letters that end up in the wastebasket, I decide to pretend that she is here with me in the Pink Palace, lying on the hot-pink bedspread with her shoes kicked off—the way Anna Maria does. This is good. It feels more normal. Now I'm ready. As I talk out loud I'll write my words down on the paper. Sometimes I amaze myself with my lightbulb of good ideas. Okay, Possible Future First Lady of the United States of America, I'm ready. Here goes!

ABIGAIL LEAH SHAPIRO

October 15, 1959

Dear Mrs. Jacqueline Lee Bouvier Kennedy,
    Hi. I hope you don't mind if right
off the bat I call you Jackie. No offense,
but Jacqueline Lee Bouvier Kennedy is a

---

mouthful. It takes an awfully long time to write it out then check for spelling mistakes. My name is Abigail Leah Shapiro, and I am in sixth grade. I think we have a lot in common.

1. We both have short versions of our names. Your real name is Jacqueline, but everybody calls you Jackie. My real name is Abigail, but everybody calls me Abby. Everybody except one really dumb boy in class who calls me Scooter Pie.
2. Our middle names are almost identical. If you say Lee and Leah really fast, you can barely hear the difference.
3. We both have houses in Massachusetts. It's called the Bay State. I bet you already know that.
4. My family thinks your husband is a very good senator and would make a good president. I'm sure you think the same thing, too.
5. My Auntie Rina says that you are a slave to fashion. Me too! I love to design beautiful clothes.

Anyway, if your husband runs for president, you will need lots of changes of outfits. So this is what I suggest. Let me be your personal fashion designer. I have so many ideas that I can't sketch them fast enough. I might only be eleven years old, but I just know in my young growing bones that my creations are perfect for you.

So here are some high-fashion designs I made just for you. I hope you like them. The first one is a plaid skirt with a matching vest. I think you could wear a sweater underneath when the weather gets cooler. The outfit looks a lot like one of my new back-to-school outfits. My skirt and vest set is a purple and sky-blue plaid. I imagine that yours is, too. I wore mine on class-picture day. It was a good choice because this year was the first year in our school that the pictures were in color. The purple and blue showed up really nice. My mother even bought the whole package. Usually she just buys the wallet-size pictures.

I also wore the outfit to synagogue for Rosh Hashanah. That's the Jewish New Year, in case you didn't know. We wish everyone who is Jewish a sweet New Year, then we eat apples dipped in honey. That's one of our customs. Sometimes I skip the apples and go straight for the honey.

I know that you are Catholic and go to church. I've been to church before with my best friend, Anna Maria Tucci, when she had her First Communion. The inside of the church was really beautiful, with the high ceilings and all those colorful stained glass windows. But the seats were hard. They hurt my tush just like the seats we sit on in synagogue. I don't think we're supposed to be comfortable when we pray.

Back to clothes! The other design is a cream-colored suit with a bright red blouse underneath. I gave the blouse a bow because I think you would look good in bows. I also think both outfits are very stylish. I really hope you like them and will want to wear them in the new decade. That's all everyone is talking about. Can you believe that in a few months it will be 1960 and the beginning of a new decade?

Bye!
Your Friend in Fashion,
Abigail Leah Shapiro (But please call me Abby)

P.S. In case you're wondering why your hair looks so puffy in the skirt-and-vest design, it's because I pretended you went to sleep with big rollers in your hair.

P.P.S. The sketches I'm sending you were traced from my sketchbook. Auntie Rina once told me that a professional designer must always keep the originals. So I traced them for you. I hope you don't mind. I also didn't color them in. I used to do that all the time for my paper doll designs. But filling everything in with colored pencils makes my hand cramp. And besides, Auntie Rina also told me that the real fashion designers in Paris and New York never color in their sketches. They see the colors in their minds. Don't worry, I've got a rainbow of colors in my mind. Trust me, I live and breathe fashion, and if you hire me, you'll find that out for yourself soon enough. You won't be sorry!

P.P.P.S. The name of my business is Abilea Coutures. Since I am a new designer, I am much cheaper than all those guys from Paris. I only charge fifteen cents for each design or twenty-five cents for two. A bargain!

7

Sweater Sets Are All the Rage

I address my first letter to Jackie in care of Senator John Fitzgerald Kennedy's office in Washington, DC, our nation's capital. I know the address is correct because Anna Maria Tucci's father looked it up for me. He should know because he works at the main post office downtown. Mr. Tucci told me to be patient. It might take a long while before Mrs. Kennedy gets the letter because of the ton of mail the senator receives every day.

I use my very best cursive penmanship when I write the letter, both inside on my Abigail Leah Shapiro pink stationery and outside when I address the envelope. I bring the letter to the kitchen and put it on top of the pile of outgoing mail. Mummy goes to the main post office every day to drop off our mail and to pick up the new stuff that's in our box. She lifts my envelope and examines it front and back.

"What's this, a letter to Mrs. Jacqueline Lee Bouvier Kennedy?" Mummy asks.

"Yup. That's what the address says."

"Why are you mailing her a letter?"

"I'm sending her samples of my fashion designs," I announce proudly.

"YOU'RE WHAT?"

"I'm letting her know that I design beautiful clothes," I say. "She might want to know."

"Oh, Abby, this is foolishness, *narishkayt*. You're a little girl. Why would a woman as famous and important as Jacqueline Kennedy want to see your sketches, not that they aren't wonderful, mind you."

"Gee, thanks so much for the compliment," I say. "Do me a favor and just mail my letter. You know, Mr. Tucci told me and Anna Maria that you can get arrested for messing with somebody's mail."

Mummy sighs one of her deep sighs and wipes her hands on her apron.

"Look, Abby, I'm sorry. I didn't mean to insult you. It's just that it's highly unlikely you'll ever get an answer back from Mrs. Kennedy. I hope you realize that. But for the record, what exactly did you say to her in your letter, if you don't mind my asking."

Actually, I do mind her asking. After her uninvited comments I feel it's none of her beeswax. If I tell her of my plans for Abilea Coutures, I'll have to listen to more of her screechy voice: "YOU WHAT! YOU WANT TO CHARGE JACQUELINE KENNEDY MONEY? WHAT'S THE MATTER WITH YOU? MAYBE YOU NEED YOUR HEAD EXAMINED."

So Mummy leaves me no choice. I lie. Just a little one.

"You don't need to go all ape on me," I say. "This is something for school. Yuh, it's a pen pal assignment. Miss Burns says we can write letters to anybody. It could be a friend, or a cousin, or a famous person. We just have to tell them about ourselves in perfect letter form."

"Well, why didn't you pick someone who you knew would answer you back? That makes more sense to me," Mummy says. "Isn't that the whole point of having a pen pal?"

"I like to aim high," I answer.

"Well, good for you," Mummy says.

"You don't sound like you mean it."

Mummy sighs again.

"And while we're on the subject, news flash, I'm not a little girl. I need a bra. I'm not going to hold out much longer for you. I'll have to take matters into my own hands."

"Here we go again," Mummy says.

"You know," I tell her, "this is America, where people have freedom to make choices for themselves."

"Who are you quoting, President Eisenhower?" she asks.

"No. I'm quoting Auntie Rina."

"*Genug*, Abby. End of discussion! I will buy you a bra when you need one and not one minute sooner. I am the mother here and I know best!"

That's it. I'll show her. I wasn't planning to write to Jackie again until I heard back from her. But since I have two extrabeautiful outfits waiting for her, I decide to send off another letter pronto. Since Mummy is not going to the post office until later today, that gives me plenty of time. Back to the Pink Palace I go to write to Jackie. This letter will not be as hard to write as the first one. We already broke the ice. Maybe we're not palsy-walsy yet, but I feel like we will be soon enough.

ABIGAIL LEAH SHAPIRO

October 16, 1959

Dear Jackie,

How are you? I am fine, thank you very much. I just wrote to you last night and I know you haven't received it yet, because Mummy hasn't been to the post office today to mail it. So, I guess you'll get two letters at once. If you're wondering why I didn't wait to hear back from you before writing another letter, here's the answer—I couldn't help myself. Mummy always says I have no impulse control.

Ta-da! Jackie, have you heard the latest fashion news flash? Sweater sets are all the rage. All the ladies are wearing them. Don't you worry, Jackie. I will not let you be left out in the cold. Here are two brand-new designs from Abilea Coutures exclusively for you!

The first outfit is a straight dark green skirt with a black watch-plaid sweater. I have a kilt that's black watch-plaid, but I don't like wearing it much. Oh, I like the pattern of the plaid and all, it's just that the big safety pin in the front of the skirt keeps opening and stabs me in the thigh. It gets right into the skin because I wear the skirt with kneesocks. Maybe I should wear it with tights instead.

The second outfit is a bit more dressy. Please notice, Jackie, that the navy-blue skirt has a little bouncy thing at the bottom and is worn with a matching navy-blue knit shell. The cardigan is something special! Just look at how I made it a cutaway sweater. I don't even know if such a thing exists yet in fashion. I told you I was filled with loads of good ideas. The sweater is pale yellow with cantaloupe-orange stars on it. I had to look up the spelling of the word "cantaloupe" in my junior dictionary. It beats me how some kids can read a book or write a letter without a dictionary close by.

Anyway, you might think the stars look a little bit like jumping jacks, but they're not. At first I thought I should make the stars all different colors, but then I said to myself, "No, Abby, do not do that! Jackie would never wear something so loud and uncouth."

I will wait patiently to hear your opinions about my designs. My Auntie Rina told me that if you buy a skirt without a sweater or a sweater without a skirt, you'll never wear the clothes. They'll hang in your closet until the cows come home. It is so important to be coordinated. That is my motto here at Abilea Coutures. I just wanted to spell that out for you in case you didn't totally get my drift by looking at the sketches. Okay, so now you've got four new outfits. Wear them in good health. That's what Auntie Rina always says to me when I get new clothes.

Bye!
Your Friend in Fashion,
Abby Shapiro

P.S. Has Senator Kennedy decided yet if he's going to run for president? If I was the first to know, I could tell everyone in my class on a Friday morning. That's when my teacher, Miss Burns, discusses current events, then leaves time for "personal events." I think by the time you get to sixth grade, you are too old for show-and-tell, so it just becomes "tell." If I had the scoop before it hit the newspapers, I could rub Susie Applegate's nose right in it. She's a jerk in my class who always tries to rank me out. So please let me know as soon as you find out. Deal?

P.P.S. I don't know what kind of shoes you like, so I gave you simple black patent leather pumps with low heels. Auntie Rina says that you are tall, so you probably don't wear spikes. Barbie wears spikes all the time. I don't have a Barbie doll yet, so I'm working as a fashion designer to earn the money. Anna Maria Tucci's Nonna Adelaide bought three designs for Barbie doll clothes. I gave her a big discount. I charged her twenty-five cents for three, so she got one design for free. If you like, I could offer you the same deal. As of today, I have a buck sixty-five in my Barbie doll fund. Only a buck thirty-five to go!

P.P.P.S. If you buy my fashion designs, I'd be very happy to keep a running tally for you, like a charge account. That's what we do for the best customers in our shoe store. So far your bill is forty cents if you want all four outfits. That's because you get the three-for-two special at twenty-five cents, plus one for fifteen cents.

P.P.P.P.S. If you ever want to discuss your account, you can call me at Juniper 3-0408.

P.P.P.P.P.S. Jackie, I'd like to ask you a personal question, if that's okay with you. How old were you when you got your first bra?

8

Witches' Brew on the Avenue

"Abby, hurry up."

Marty is on the porch waiting for me so we can go trick-or-treating and a little something else.

"I'll be right there," I yell back.

I was in the kitchen but I forgot Mei, so I ran to my bedroom to get her.

My Halloween costume this year is red Chinese silk pajamas, just like it was for the last few years. Anna Maria Tucci's Nonna Adelaide sewed them for me so my Chinese rag doll, Mei, and I could be dressed like twins. Auntie Rina and Mummy offered to pay, but Nonna Adelaide refused to hear of it.

"Abby's like a second granddaughter to me," she said.

The pajamas could be used for sleeping, but they are more like a lounging outfit. So far Nonna Adelaide has sewed two pairs since Mei came to live with me. She made each pair with one extra-deep pocket so Mei could fit comfortably inside and go with me wherever I go.

There are lots of reasons why Mei is my favorite foreign doll. For example, she's very beautiful, with black pigtails and a little red-stitched mouth. The lady who brought her to me from China told me that she would be my good luck doll. She said, "This doll is dressed all in red, which means good luck in Chinese culture.

Take good care of her and she'll bring you happiness for the rest of your life." But there is another important reason why Mei is my favorite. She was made by Chinese orphans, so I have a lot of responsibility to love and protect her.

"Okay, I'm here. I'm ready now," I say as I walk onto the porch.

My brother gives me a dirty look. He's shifting his weight from one foot to the other. He's wearing his khaki-green army jacket and a metal helmet. There's camouflage greasepaint smeared all over his face, neck, and hands. My mother thinks he's in costume for Halloween, but he's not. Marty's dressed for combat.

"Have a good time," Mummy says. "But don't stay out too late. There are a lot of unsavory types wandering the streets on Halloween night."

"Okay, Mum," I say. "I'll bring you back some good candy."

We leave the porch, but when we hear her close the kitchen door, we sneak back into the garage. That's where we've stashed our pillowcases, supplies, and the pair of dungarees I'll wear over my pajama bottoms.

"Shaving cream?" Marty asks.

"Check."

"Eggs?"

"Check."

When Marty planned this military operation, he wrote down the supplies he'd need on a piece of paper. Then he asked me to take it to De Luca's Market and buy the stuff. That way Mrs. De Luca wouldn't suspect that Marty was buying the stuff for Halloween pranks. Otherwise, she'd call up my mother to double-check if the eggs and shaving cream really were on her shopping list. If that happened, Marty would have been in hot water and the mission would have been scrapped.

Buying the stuff set me back one dollar and twelve cents from my Barbie doll fund. But I didn't complain to Marty or ask for the money back. He's so good to me, I'd do anything for him. For the past week I hid the shaving cream in my bedroom on the top shelf of my closet and the eggs down in the basement boiler room. I moved everything to the garage today while the family was at work.

"Flashlight?" I ask Marty.

"Check."

"Canteen?"

"Check."

"Filled with Kool-Aid™?"

"Affirmative."

The Kool-Aid is not exactly a supply for the mission. It's in case we get thirsty.

"Swiss army knife?" I ask.

"Affirmative, again."

"What do we need the knife for?"

"In case."

"In case of what?"

"Just in case," he answers. "Don't question your superior officer."

"Fine. What about the walkie-talkies?"

Marty nods.

"You have to say affirmative, or else it won't be official," I tell him.

Marty groans. "Affirmative."

Marty has all of this survival gear because he's a Boy Scout.

"Okay, General, let's go over the plan," I say to my brother.

Marty pushes back the cuff of his jacket to look at his watch. It's an official World War II army-issued model that he bought at a pawn shop with some of his Bar Mitzvah money. He was only allowed to spend a little bit of the gift money because ninety-eight percent of it has to stay in the bank and grow interest for his college fund.

"At present it is exactly nineteen hundred hours," Marty whispers. "That gives us time to sweep the entire neighborhood for candy before we rendezvous with the troops at twenty thirty hours."

Marty holds the pillowcase for the candy and sticks the can of shaving cream in an inside pocket of his army jacket. I carry the eggs in my pillowcase, but they're inside a plastic box for safety.

"Whatever you do," Marty says, "do not drop those eggs. That's precious cargo you're transporting, Private."

I stick my tongue out at my brother.

"Give me some credit, will ya? Who's the one who had the brilliant idea to keep the eggs in the boiler room so they'd get nice and ripe?"

"Okay, okay," Marty says.

Marty might be the commanding officer, but he looks a little nervous to me. I'm not. I'm as cool as a cucumber. "Tell me again which troops are coming," I say, even though I already know the answer.

"Harry and Todd," Marty says.

"Did you say Barry and Bob?"

I'm goofing on Marty to give him the chance to speak in military language. He plays along.

"Listen up, Private," he commands. "I said Harry... Hotel-Alpha-Romeo-Romeo-Yankee. And Todd...Tango-Oscar-Delta-Delta. Got it?"

"Yes, sir, General Marty, sir," I answer with a salute.

We start out on Darlene Avenue. But we probably won't stop at too many houses. We live on a loser street as far as Halloween candy goes.

"Mrs. Lazarus?" I ask.

"Sure," Marty says. "Her porch light is on."

Mrs. Lazarus leaves out a pail of candy bars with a note on the door. "Honor system. Help yourselves to one chocolate bar per person." But somebody wasn't too honest this year. It's early and the pail's been cleaned out.

"Mrs. Whelan?"

"No way. The house is pitch-black."

We ring the bell at Mr. Lane's house. He's not home, but his mother is there to hand out candy. She talks to us a bit and gives each of us four big lollipops. Marty and I decide not to ring any more bells on our street. The pickings are crummy. There's the family with the twins next door, but they eat all the good stuff themselves and give the trick-or-treaters the leftover pieces. Then there's Mrs. Feinstein, a lady who looks like a man because she has a mustache. Marty doesn't want to go there. He says she gives him the creeps. And besides, last year she gave out candy apples that she made herself. Mummy made us toss them in the trash because she says never eat anything unwrapped from her house. She says Mrs. Feinstein is no *baleboste*, no homemaker. She has a cat that drags its bottom along the kitchen counter, where she prepares food. Mummy knows this because she was inside the house when she went to collect for the March of Dimes and saw with her own two eyes. Mummy absolutely hates cats. She says they're sneaky and will suffocate you when you sleep. That's in addition to giving you worms.

There's a nice Greek family at the end of the street. They give out yummy homemade honey cookies instead of candy. I really want some of those cookies because I love honey. But Marty says we can't go there either, because the honey will get all over my fingers and I can't have sticky fingers tonight.

We turn left on to Malvern Road. It's a big street with houses crammed in tight next to each other. Trick-or-treaters are everywhere. I hate it when kids from other neighborhoods find out which streets are not loser streets. Then their parents drive them here and trail behind them in their cars. Don't they have good neighborhoods of their own?

At the end of Malvern, we make a left onto Spring Street. After we ring bells on Spring, we turn right onto West Street. Marty shines the flashlight at his watch.

"It's twenty fifteen. Just a few more houses, Abby. The guys will be waiting. The pillowcase is pretty full of candy, anyway."

We backtrack to Spring Street. Harry Degen's house is the third one down on the right. Harry's backyard is really big and connects up to the witches' house on Darlene Avenue through some woods.

"This mission is all about the wiffle balls, right?" I ask my brother.

"They steal them, and they have no right to do that," he says. "And besides, they give Harry's father a hard time. We're just gonna give them what's owed them."

Harry's father owns only one-half acre of the woods and the witches own five and one-half. Mr. Degen wants to buy all the land from the witches so he can put up some houses and make a killing. But the witches won't budge even though he's offered them all kinds of money. They just want to keep the woods, the woods.

Harry and Todd are waiting for us inside the Degens' garage. Marty flicks the flashlight twice through the side door window, which is the signal that we're coming in. Harry and Todd are sitting in the dark inside Harry's mother's Buick™ sedan. His parents are away on vacation in Puerto Rico and his grandmother is staying with him. Harry told Marty not to worry about her, because she's as deaf as a doorpost and will never figure out a thing. Marty keeps his flashlight on, pointing down to the ground so I won't fall and ruin the whole mission.

"Crud," Todd says. "Does she really have to come along?"

"No insubordination, Colonel Silver," Marty says. "There's no way we can successfully pull off this mission without Private Abby."

I like how Marty puts him in his place. That's family loyalty for you! I stick my tongue out at Todd and mouth "Shut up, Todd." He's going to hate me even more after tonight when Marty promotes me to lieutenant.

We all wait inside the Buick. Marty checks his watch from time to time. When it is twenty-one hundred hours, Marty opens the backseat door and tells us to prepare.

"Any final words, soldiers?" he asks.

Harry and Todd just shake their heads. I can tell they're scared.

"Let's do it, General," I say, looking at Todd. "I'm no chicken, like some people I know."

Marty leaves our pillowcase full of candy in the Buick. We'll come back for it later. I take the carton of eggs and give my pillowcase to Marty. He'll need it for our rescue mission. Marty gives the command to get into formation. He leads the brigade through Harry's backyard and into the woods. Marty puts up his hand for us to stop when we come to the other side of the woods. Quietly he gives me the walkie-talkie and the can of shaving cream. I nod. It's now or never. It's do or die.

Marty and Harry crouch down behind some bushes at the edge of the woods. They'll wait there until I call for them. Todd runs off behind some other bushes to pee. All of Darlene Avenue is quiet. There are no last-minute trick-or-treaters. That's the good thing about living on a loser street. It's dark because house porch lights are already turned off, and also because we have no streetlamps and the sky is cloudy. The conditions are perfect for Operation Whiskey-India-Tango-Charlie-Hotel-Echo-Sierra.

I drop belly-down and slowly worm my way on the grass from the edge of the woods onto the lawn of the big white Victorian house. I keep the carton of eggs on the grass in front of me and carefully slide it up as I wriggle like a snake. I'm fast and make it up to the big wraparound porch in lickety-split time. I see the big metal pail straight ahead. It's huge, like the kind I saw at a farm that was used to collect milk.

I move up a few more feet and whisper into the walkie-talkie. "Now!" The soldiers get into position as I stick my hand into the metal pail and perfect-pitch the fifteen wiffle balls that the witches have stolen from us. The guys catch them one by one and load them into the pillowcase.

Now it's shaving cream time. I shake it up real good and spray the metal pail as well as the rocking chairs and the front door. The can empties faster than I expect. I dump it in the metal can.

Mistake! Big mistake! I shouldn't have done that. The metal shaving cream can clangs against the metal pail. Marty hears it and says through the walkie-talkie, "Mission over, retreat!" But not me. I will not waste those eggs. Quickly I pitch one right after another all over the door and windows. Gunk drips down on the windowsills and over the brooms perched on the porch. The smell is so bad, I gag. I reach down for my last two eggs when I hear Marty yell, "DANGER!"

The porch light turns on, the front door flings wide open, and a bony witch arm touches the back of my jacket. No way I'm going to be taken prisoner and skinned alive. I chuck the last two rotten eggs over my shoulder and run like the dickens.

At the edge of the lawn, Marty grabs my hand. We escape with Harry and Todd back through the woods. We don't stop until we're safe inside the Buick.

"Great work, Abby," Marty says, still panting.

Harry nods in agreement.

"What about you, Todd," I say. "Cat got your tongue?"

"Okay, okay, thanks, Abby," Todd says.

"That's Lieutenant Abby to you," I say to the boys. "And don't you forget that I'm a permanent member of the army now!"

We sit in the backseat of Harry Degen's mother's Buick until our hearts stop thumping. Marty opens the canteen and we take turns swigging the Kool-Aid. I go first because I saved the day, and also this way I won't have to worry about wiping down after Todd takes his slug.

"Let's go, Abby," Marty says. "We'll go down West Street two extra blocks and cut through backyards to get home."

Marty opens the car door.

"Wait. You're forgetting something, General," I say.

"Oh yuh, the candy," Marty says.

"No, that's not what I mean. I mean the oath. We all have to swear, pinky swear, that we'll never tell anybody what happened tonight."

I say that to let them know I'm no rat. I'd never fink out on the army. But that's not the real reason. I want it to be a secret because I'm already ashamed of what I've done. Why did I pitch rotten eggs at some old lady? What kind of horrible kid does stuff like that? Witch or no witch, it was wrong. I wonder if Marty is feeling the same way that I do.

"She's right," Todd says.

"Okay," Marty says. "On the count of three."

We each put our right pinkies in the center and lock them tight. We squeeze our eyes shut and tug our pinkies as hard as we can without breaking apart. Good. Now it's sealed forever and ever.

9
Uncle Max Talks Back

"Did you realize there was a hole in your pocket?" Mummy asks on Sunday afternoon. She lays my clean folded laundry on my bed. Putting it away in my bureau drawers is one of those things I have to do for free. Her question catches me off guard.

"Huh?"

"Your Chinese pajamas. The ones you wore last night trick-or-treating. The entire pocket seam was pulled open."

I freeze with the charcoal sketching pencil in my hand and stare at the wall of hot-pink daisies in front of my desk.

"No, I didn't know about any hole," I say.

"Well, no matter. I gave them to Auntie Rina to mend," Mummy says as she shuts the door on her way out of the Pink Palace.

My heart pounds and I feel a little dizzy. And it's not because my eyes are out of focus from staring at the daisies. Where's Mei? I look up at the three rows of glass wall shelves that display my foreign doll collection. Mei is not in her space on the lowest shelf between the doll from France and the doll from Switzerland. That means I never put her away last night before I tossed the pajamas in the hamper. I get on hands and knees and look under the beds, under the shag area rugs, in the bureau, desk, closets, and in the wastebasket. Mei is nowhere to be found in the Pink Palace.

This is not good. Think, think, think. Where else could she be? What would Perry Mason and his private investigator, Paul Drake, do? Investigate, of course! I must retrace my steps.

Okay, I know I ran back to the Pink Palace to put Mei in my pocket before Marty and I went trick-or-treating. So when we left the house, I know for one hundred percent certain that she was in my pocket. Then...and then I don't know. I have no idea if the seam was open from the start, or if I made it happen when I shoved the can of shaving cream underneath the waistband of my dungarees. Did Mei fall out on Darlene Avenue, somewhere else in the neighborhood, or in the woods?

The only thing I know for sure is the very horrible truth that Mei, my favorite, special, good luck doll, might be gone forever. I made a promise to look after her always, and I didn't check on Mei even once last night. I was too busy thinking about Operation Whiskey-India-Tango-Charlie-Hotel-Echo-Sierra and pleasing Marty.

But wait! Maybe, just maybe, there's one teensy-weensy chance that Mei isn't lost. Maybe she was still in the pocket. Maybe Auntie Rina has her upstairs and is waiting for me to collect her.

I run up the front staircase and into the second-floor living room. Auntie Rina is lying on the sofa with her ankles crisscrossed reading the Sunday newspapers. Her slippers are off and I can see the bunion on her right foot.

"Oh, Abby," Auntie Rina says. "I fixed your pajamas and left them on the dining room table. Let me tell you, that was some hole."

Hope slips down the drain.

I plop down on one of the goose feather–filled cushions.

I have to go outside right now and search for Mei before it gets dark. I bounce up from the sofa two seconds after I sit down.

"Abby, what's with the *shpilkes*?" Auntie Rina asks. "You look like you're sitting on pins and needles."

"Nope. I'm fine. I just think I'll take a walk. You know, get some fresh air in my lungs."

We hear a car horn blast from the driveway. I run to the window to check it out.

"It's Uncle Max and Sy," I tell Auntie Rina. "They're both getting out of the car."

"Oh, for heaven's sakes," Auntie Rina says. "What does he have to *shlep* him inside the house for?"

Auntie Rina acts annoyed, but she flattens out the wrinkles in her housedress as she steps into her slippers. Then she turns her back to me, fluffs her hair, and sticks her hand in her pocket. She thinks I don't know what she's doing, but I do. She's touching up her lipstick. She can put it on perfectly without a mirror. Then she blots her lips with a handkerchief that looks like it's plastered with wall-to-wall S.W.A.K. lip stickers that I put on the back of Valentine's Day cards.

"Hey, Uncle Max," I say as he walks into the upstairs living room.

"Hay is for horses," he answers.

I don't know my Uncle Max as well as I do my Uncle Morris. Uncle Max only hangs out with me in short hunks of time. Auntie Rina says that as far as him and me and the rest of the family are concerned, we're like ships that pass each other in the dead of night or at the crack of dawn. Or something like that.

Sy is trailing behind Uncle Max, but he stands at least a foot taller. They remind me of Mutt and Jeff from the funnies. Uncle Max dresses even spiffier than Mr. Lane across the street. He's wearing a dark burgundy silk sports jacket, and his shoes are polished so shiny, they give off a glow. Uncle Max has a habit of smoothing back his hair, both hands at once, even though there isn't much hair left to smoothe.

"Hi, Sy," I say.

Sy smiles and nods a hello. Sy is a shy guy. I think that he must have been the most polite inmate in prison. Maybe the warden let him out early for good manners. Sy removes his hat before he speaks to Auntie Rina. I think that's very gentlemanly of him. Sy has lots of hair. And it's thick and black without any gray. Not even at the temples.

"Hello, Rina. It's very nice to see you. How is your health?" Sy asks.

"Can't complain," she says. "And you?"

"I'm managing," Sy answers. "Thank you for asking."

"You're quite welcome. Would you like a cup of tea?"

Auntie Rina sounds so formal, like she's meeting Sy for the first time when actually they've known each other forever.

"We're not staying," Uncle Max says. "I just came by to pick up a few things."

"Oh, I see how it is," Auntie Rina says. "You'd rather be elsewhere than spend a minute with your family."

Sy looks down at the olive-green wall-to-wall carpeting like he was the one who was yelled at. Uncle Max sidesteps Auntie Rina and goes down the hallway to the bedroom he shares with Uncle Morris. He comes back out with a thick envelope. It's filled with cold, hard cash. Sometimes Uncle Max uses his bureau as a bank instead of the nightly deposit box.

"I suppose you're going to spend that on Miss What's-Her-Name. Let me guess. What did she ask for...a mink coat, diamond earrings?" Auntie Rina says. "You know, Max, you're not a youngster anymore. It's high time you stopped being played the fool by these gold diggers."

"You never change, do you, Rina?" Uncle Max snaps. "Still trying to run everybody's life."

"I'm only looking out for you," Auntie Rina says. "That's what family does for one another."

"Let's get one thing straight. I don't need your help."

Auntie Rina's mouth purses like a prune.

"For the last time, her name is Dolores. Get used to it because she's the one for me. And as far as this goes," Uncle Max says, holding up the envelope, "the dough is down payment on a house. Dolores and I are moving in together. Permanently."

First Auntie Rina gasps, then she balls up her fist and pounds her chest.

"*A klog iz mir!*" she wails.

I think saying "woe is me" is a bit dramatic.

"See ya later, alligator," Uncle Max says to me. He ignores Auntie Rina.

"After a while, crocodile," I answer.

He pinches my cheek and I spot a ring with a big red star ruby on his right pinkie finger. "Wow! That's huge!" I say.

Uncle Max winks at me and says, "I found it. It's my lucky ring."

"Really, you found it?"

This gives me hope that I might find Mei.

"He didn't find it. He won it playing poker," Auntie Rina yells. "He won it off one of the bums he hangs out with at the club."

Uncle Max tugs down the shirt sleeves under his burgundy silk sports jacket so he can adjust his cuff links. The color of the jacket matches his new pinkie ring.

"Let's go, Sy," he says. "I don't want to keep Dolores waiting any longer than necessary," Uncle Max says as he looks Auntie Rina straight in the eyeballs.

"Is she at the Pink Elephant?" I ask.

"That's right, kiddo," Uncle Max answers.

The Pink Elephant is the name of Uncle Max's nightclub. I didn't copy him when I named my bedroom the Pink Palace. Hot pink has always been my favorite color. The name of the nightclub means that if you drink too much liquor, you might see crazy things, like a pink elephant in the room. I guess it's no different than when Mrs. Whelan walked down Darlene Avenue thinking she was Miss America. Anyway, Uncle Max opened his nightclub during Prohibition, when it was illegal to serve liquor at a bar. But he served it anyway. According to my brother, Marty, that's when Uncle Max became a gangster. Marty called him a bootlegger.

"Wait!" I say as I tug at the back of Uncle Max's jacket. "Do you think I could meet Dolores someday?"

"Sure, kid. Why not? In fact, she's dying to meet you and your brother."

"Really?"

Auntie Rina mumbles something in Yiddish that I think is the equivalent of "over my dead body."

Sy says something back to her in Yiddish, but he says it so fast, I can't pick out any words. Uncle Max shoots Auntie Rina a dirty look.

"You know what, Abby? There's no time like the present. Let's go. I'm taking you with me down to the club right now," Uncle Max says.

I've been to the Pink Elephant loads of times. It's on the whole fifth floor of a building downtown that overlooks the parkway. Marty and I used to go all the time when we were younger to watch the city parades. You get the best view from the nightclub's big front windows. But I haven't been back since two Fourth of Julys ago. Uncle Max got angry with us because we had a spraying fight with the seltzer nozzles.

"It's okay, Auntie Rina. Just tell Mummy where I went."

Before Auntie Rina can put up a fuss, I kiss her and whisper, "Don't worry, I still love you" in her ear.

Uncle Max heads downstairs first.

"Get Abby home by a reasonable hour," Auntie Rina shouts. "Don't forget she's got school tomorrow."

"And don't forget I'll be back next week for the rest of my things," Uncle Max shouts back.

I get as far as the fourth step on the staircase when I realize that Sy is not behind me. He's still upstairs in the living room with Auntie Rina. I hear them talking, and by the sound of Auntie Rina's voice, I guess that she's still burning mad. I tiptoe back up the staircase and eavesdrop from the kitchen.

"Stop asking me, Sy," Auntie Rina says. "This is getting to be ridiculous already."

"What's ridiculous?" Sy asks. "That I care for you? That I've always cared for you? All I'm asking is to take you to dinner."

"It's too late for all that nonsense. *Genug!* Stop asking me because it simply is not possible. It wasn't possible forty years ago and it's not possible now."

Sy has been in love with my Auntie Rina for *forty* years? In Sunday school Rabbi Levine taught us that that's how long Moses wandered in the desert. Sy might be even more lovesick for Auntie Rina than Miss Burns is for Mr. Polonski. This is one big fat secret. But Auntie Rina must like Sy, too, otherwise she wouldn't have primped and put on lipstick before he and Uncle Max came upstairs. Now I'm more curious than ever. I really need to know what the true story is between these two, but I'll have to be careful. If I come right out and ask Auntie Rina, she'll get mad and never tell.

"Why not?" Sy asks. "Give me one good reason."

Wow, that is pretty bold talk for Sy, the shy guy.

"Because I said so. That's reason enough."

That sounds so gruff and cruel.

"You're breaking my heart," Sy says.

"Oh, stop. I've had enough *tsuris* for one day."

I hear Sy's footsteps coming down the staircase and scoot outside ahead of him. I feel bad. I hope that Sy, the shy guy, the driver guy, the gangster guy, doesn't become Sy, the crying guy.

10
Looking for Mei

Sy backs down the driveway in Uncle Max's brand-new black DeSoto Firedome™ convertible. The car has big rear fins that make it look like a rocket ship. Because autumn is when the new models come out, Uncle Max gets a good deal right off the lot on one of last season's cars. He buys a car every October, which means that his cars never get a chance to lose that new-car smell. But Uncle Max doesn't like to drive, so Sy does it for him. Uncle Max has a driver's license though, but only for identification purposes. He says that every now and then you have to prove who you are. He means to the cops.

"So what do you think, kid?" Uncle Max asks.

"She's a beaut all right," I say. "Much nicer than last year's hardtop."

"I thought so, too," he says.

I wish Uncle Max would tell Sy to drop the convertible top so it would feel like we're flying through the air like Superman. But it's too cold for that now. Today is the first of November. The weatherman said people should bring in any outdoor plants on account of it might frost.

"Uncle Max, I'm in hot water," I say.

I've got the whole big backseat to myself. Uncle Max drapes one arm over the back of his seat as he turns to face me. He runs his hand back and forth over the leather upholstery like he's petting a puppy. Uncle Max's hands look a lot nicer than mine. My one bad habit is chewing my cuticles, so I always have hangnails that look like fringe. Uncle Max's fingernails are buffed and perfectly filed. That's courtesy of Agnes, the beautician. Her husband owed Uncle Max some serious money, so the debt got paid with a lifetime's promise of shaves, haircuts, and manicures. I guess he needs nice hands to deal cards. Uncle Max still leaves Agnes a huge tip every time he's in her shop.

"You and me both, kid," Uncle Max says. "I'm always in hot water with your Auntie Rina. She still thinks I'm her kid brother and has to watch over my every move."

Sy doesn't flinch. He's as cool as a cucumber at the mention of Auntie Rina's name. I don't see any goose bumps pimpling on the back of his thick neck.

"No, that's not what I mean," I say. "I'm really in trouble."

"Sy, pull over," Uncle Max orders.

Sy steers to the side of Darlene Avenue across from the big white Victorian house and moves the gearshift into park. I look across the street at the witches' house. It shows no signs of our raid. The windows are sparkling clean, and there's not a trace of egg or shaving cream.

"What's the problem, Abby?" Uncle Max asks.

"Remember my little Chinese doll, the very first one I got for my foreign doll collection?"

"Sure thing."

Uncle Max nods like he knows what I'm talking about, but I don't think he does. He's just trying to be a good listener.

"Well, I lost her last night trick-or-treating. I shouldn't have taken her out with me, but I did, and it's making me sick that she might be gone forever. You see I had her in my . . ."

I stop talking because I see the witches come outside through their front door. They grab their brooms and start sweeping the porch. What's wrong with these people? Why are they always sweeping?

"Abby?"

I point across the street.

"Oh yuh, sorry. Hey, Uncle Max, do you know those two witches?"

"They're not witches. They're two old women from the Old Country."

I can't believe what Uncle Max says.

"What! The Old Country? You mean they're Jewish and had to run away in the middle of the night like you did?"

"No, they're not Jewish. They're Polish or Lithuanian peasants. They're simple women who keep to themselves. They don't bother anybody," Uncle Max says.

"Well, they bother Marty and his friends," I say.

Uncle Max puffs up a bit, and Sy turns around from the driver's seat.

"What do you mean? In what way do they bother them?"

"Well, they collect the stray wiffle balls for one thing. They keep them in a big pail by the front door."

"Did anyone ask for them back?"

"No! Are you kidding! Nobody dares. They're scary looking and their bodies are crooked. One of them drags a leg when she walks and the other one has an arm without a hand. And besides, Harry Degen said that kids who get too close to them have disappeared then ended up in a pot of witches' brew with rats, snails, and lost puppies."

Sy laughs. It's a big, roaring laugh, like a Papa Bear laugh. It's catchy and makes me laugh a little bit, too. I bet Sy also has a nice singing voice.

"Oh, come on now, Abby," Uncle Max says.

"You never know. It could be true. Auntie Rina calls them witches in Yiddish and always say *feh* whenever she passes their house. She says that they should go back to where they came from and stay there for good. She wouldn't say that unless they were bad people. She never talks down about anybody she doesn't know. Auntie Rina always says that in this life you have to give people the benefit of the doubt before you pass judgment."

"Your Auntie Rina is a good woman, but she doesn't always practice what she preaches. She certainly hasn't given Dolores the benefit of the doubt, has she?" Uncle Max says.

I do have a bad habit of sticking my foot in my mouth.

"No, I guess she hasn't."

"Look, do you want me to send Sy across the street to get the wiffle balls?" Uncle Max asks.

"Ah, no, no, that's okay. Marty'll get them."

"So what else do they do that's so terrible?"

"You know, never mind. Forget I even mentioned the witches or the wiffle balls. It's not important. But could we drive around the neighborhood so I could look for my doll Mei?"

"Absolutely," Uncle Max says.

Sy drives slowly, and I stick my head out the open window to look. The air feels good blowing on my face, but it's just second best to how it would be to drive with the top down. We ride up and down the neighborhood streets and Sy even stops by Harry's house so I can run into the woods to look for Mei. She's nowhere along the path we took or stuck in the brush. If she were, her bright red pajamas would stick out like a sore thumb. Uncle Max says I'll have to look again tomorrow with Marty or with my friends. He wants to get back to the club.

"Sorry about your doll, kid. Them's the breaks," Uncle Max says.

"It's my fault. I should have known better."

"Chin up," Uncle Max says. "You're one tough little cookie."

"Don't worry, Abby," Sy says. "I'm sure that your doll will turn up. You have to think positive."

I don't think so, Sy. If I were a gambler like you, I'd say the odds of Mei turning up are about equal to Auntie Rina going out on a date with you.

11
The Pink Elephant

It's a short ride downtown. Sy swings around to the parkway then drives the car down the narrow alley behind Uncle Max's building. We go in through the service entrance and take the elevator up to the fifth floor. Sy, the shy guy, the driver guy, the gangster guy, the in-love-with-Auntie-Rina guy, is also the elevator guy. He drives that elevator just as smoothly as he drives the DeSoto Firedome.

Sy doesn't have a house of his own, so Uncle Max gave him an apartment on the fourth floor. Uncle Max rents out some of the space on the other floors for offices. He says it pays for the taxes and upkeep.

As soon as the gated elevator door opens, I hear singing and piano music. We walk three across, me in the middle, down the hallway and through the double milk-glass doors into the Pink Elephant. Right off the bat I see there are new things going on since the last time I was here. First, there's a whole pile of tools and wires and light fixtures in boxes. A big section of the gray swirly linoleum floor has been ripped up and a wooden plank floor is being laid in its place. Second, there's a shiny black baby grand piano backed into a corner of the club. There never used to be a piano in the club, just a long oak wood bar, bar stools, folding tables and chairs for poker. It looks like the Pink Elephant is getting spruced up. And then, of course, there is the woman at the piano who must be Dolores.

She stops playing and stands up the second we walk in. Dolores is beautiful. She's made up with lots of liner and blue shadow to match her eyes. Her mouth is puckered into the shape of a heart and is colored in with pink frosty lipstick.

"You're back!" Dolores says excitedly.

"That I am. And I brought someone special with me. Dolores, meet my niece, Abby Shapiro. Abby, meet Dolores McAffee," Uncle Max says. "I'll leave you two girls alone to get to know each other. When I'm done with business, we'll grab dinner."

I watch Sy follow Uncle Max into the back office. Dolores walks right over and hugs me big. I don't think I've ever gotten a hug before from someone I just met for the first time. But I don't mind, because this hug is a good hug, like she really means she's happy to meet me. I'm no dummy. I could tell if it was a phony hug.

"Oh, Abby, I've heard so much about you," Dolores says. "I'm so pleased to meet you."

Suddenly I feel a little shy. I don't know what to say. That's unusual for me.

"I love your haircut," I blurt out.

"Thanks, hon. I just had it done yesterday. It's the latest do. It's called a bubble cut. Your Uncle Max loves it even though at first he didn't want me to cut my hair. I've had long hair for ages, but I usually pinned it up with some tortoiseshell combs. Oh, listen to me," Dolores says, "here I go babbling on. Abby, let's talk about something more interesting. Let's talk about you."

Dolores takes my hand and leads me to the bar. I step onto the brass foot railing and boost myself up onto a bar stool. Dolores goes behind the bar to make us two Shirley Temples. I'm giddy with excitement and spin myself around.

"How many cherries?" she asks, before plunking them in the ginger ale.

"Two please," I answer.

I will never again in my whole life eat more than two cherries. That time when Marty and I had the water fight with the seltzer guns in the Pink Elephant, I also ate an entire jar of Maraschino cherries, then threw up all over the bar. Maybe that's what really made Uncle Max angry more than the puddles of seltzer.

Dolores takes two cherries for her Shirley Temple as well. Then she joins me on the other side of the bar and claims the stool next to mine. We clunk our glasses.

"Here's to our friendship," she says. "Next time hopefully I'll get to meet your brother, Marty."

"Yuh, he wasn't home when Uncle Max decided to kidnap me."

"Well, I'm glad. Oh, I mean not about Marty not being home. I meant about your kidnapping."

"I know. I understood what you meant," I say.

I do not tell Dolores that the only reason Uncle Max decided to take me to the Pink Elephant in the first place is because he was mad at Auntie Rina.

We sit for a few seconds just checking each other out. Dolores is a great smiler. She smiles big, like she's having her picture taken. Each tooth in her mouth is as pearly white as the one next to it. And there are no lipstick smudges on any of them.

"How long have you been going steady with my uncle Max?" I ask.

I hope Dolores doesn't think I'm being too pushy.

"Well, I met your uncle when I answered an advertisement he placed in the newspaper for a singer. You can see that he's doing some long overdue renovations in the club."

"Yuh, I noticed," I say.

Uncle Max never mentioned anything about this to the family.

"Well, your Uncle Max has big plans. He wants to turn the

Pink Elephant into more of a legit spot. Like a supper club. Do you know what that is?"

I shake my head side to side.

"Well, that means that the Pink Elephant will serve good food and provide entertainment for the guests. A brand-new modern kitchen will be installed in a couple of weeks. And here's the best part...there'll be a house band and I'll be at the piano singing two sets Friday and Saturday nights."

"I get it," I say. "That means if the Pink Elephant becomes a classier joint, then normal people will come here instead of card sharks, bums, and barflies."

"Oh, Abby, you're cute as a button!" Dolores says. "And to answer your question, I've been going steady with your Uncle Max since the day we met. It was love at first sight for both of us. And from what I understand, it's the same date as your birthday."

"September fourteenth!" we both say at the same time.

Dolores punches my arm lightly and says, "Jinx, you owe me a Coke™!"

"Wow, you know how to do that stuff?" I ask. "I thought only kids knew how to play that game."

I try to imagine for a moment if I did that to Mummy. She'd say, "Oh, stop it, Abby. That kind of foolishness is so unnecessary."

"Sure, I know that game," Dolores says. "I'm not *that* old."

This makes me pleased as punch. Not only are Dolores and her teeth perfect, but the fact that she and Uncle Max fell in love on my birthday gives me a good feeling. I think their romance is one of those *bashert*, "meant-to-be" things.

"What's not that old?" I ask, even though I know kids are never supposed to ask grownups their age.

"I'll be thirty-eight come Christmas day," Dolores answers.

"That's too bad," I say.

"Don't I know," Dolores says. "I always figured by this age I'd be an old married lady with lots of kids."

"Oh no, that's not what I meant. My best friend, Anna Maria Tucci, once told me that she'd hate to have a birthday on Christmas. She said it would stink because you could never have a birthday party. Nobody would come, unless all of your friends were Jewish and didn't celebrate Christmas."

Dolores reaches over and gently smoothes my hair. It feels nice.

"You're a sweetheart, just like your Uncle Max said you'd be," she says. "You know what I like about you?"

"No, what?" I ask.

"You speak your mind. You're not afraid to express your opinions."

Mummy says I have too many opinions. She says that sometimes she misses the days when I was a baby because I couldn't talk back. That makes me wonder what it would feel like to have Dolores McAffee as my mother, a young, beautiful mother. If Dolores was my mother, then Susie Applegate would be jealous like crazy because Dolores is notches higher than Susie's mother on the pretty pole. If Dolores was my mother, we'd have tons of fun shopping and having lunch at Schrafft's, sipping a vanilla frappe or a lime rickey with two straws. If Dolores was my mother, she'd be in a good mood all the time and sing and say happy things all day long. She'd be nothing like Mummy, who is always waiting for the other shoe to drop. Dolores would never tell me not to chase rainbows, because only fools believe there's a pot of gold at the end. If Dolores was my mother, she'd never walk around with a missing tooth and a ripped sweater.

"I think you look like a teenager," I tell Dolores. "I think you look like a real live Barbie doll, only with short hair."

"Why, Abby, that's a lovely compliment," she says. "I think you're very pretty, too."

"Really?"

Dolores's head tilts to one side like a dog's does when you talk to it in a high-pitched voice.

"Of course I do. I'm sure people must tell you all the time that you're a very pretty young lady."

I shrug. Mummy and Auntie Rina never tell me that I'm pretty. Ever. And if somebody else does, they quickly kill the compliment by turning their heads over their left shoulders and say, "*keynehore*, poo poo poo," then make three quick little tongue spits.

"Why do you do this to me?" I asked them once. "It's mean. Can't somebody say one nice thing about me?"

"No," Auntie Rina said. "They might really be trying to curse you and give you the evil eye."

"It's our way of protecting you," Mummy said. "You'll understand when you get older."

"That's the stupidest thing I ever heard or saw," I told them.

"No, it's not," Mummy said. "This is what your *Bubbie* Lena did in the Old Country and it's part of our traditions. If you say it's stupid, then you're being disrespectful to *Bubbie* Lena."

"*Bubbie* Lena died. Can't we retire her rules?" I asked. "Or maybe get some new ones that don't come from the Old Country?"

"Don't be sassy," Mummy said. "End of discussion."

Sometimes they change the compliment rule a little bit, but only when it's a Jewish person giving the praise. Like the time I went with Mummy across the street to visit Mrs. Lazarus and she kissed my cheeks and said in Yiddish that I had a *sheyne ponim*, a "pretty face." Mummy didn't fling her head over her shoulder to start hurling saliva, but instead said, "Abby? She's not that pretty." And Mrs. Lazarus nodded in agreement with her. Then Mrs. Lazarus said, "But she's so smart." And Mummy said, "Abby? She's not so smart." It's like some stupid private joke, only it's not funny. And why play this game at all with somebody like Mrs.

Lazarus, who I know likes me and would never curse me even a little bit in the first place?

"Do you have a Barbie doll?" Dolores asks. "I understand she's the latest rage."

"Not yet. I'm saving up for one. Mummy said I have to earn the money rather than expect to just get things. So I'm selling my fashion designs."

"You don't say," Dolores says.

"Yup. I'm going to be a fashion designer when I grow up."

"That's swell," Dolores says.

"Can you keep a secret?" I ask Dolores.

"Of course. Your secret is safe with me."

"Well, I've been designing clothes for Jacqueline Kennedy. And I'm waiting for an answer back. I sent her two letters with sketches and I'm hoping she'll buy my designs. But I know Mummy would go hog wild if she knew I asked Jackie Kennedy to pay me money for fashion designs, so I told her I was writing a letter to her for a school pen pal assignment."

"Oh, I see. Well, don't worry, my lips are sealed. It's none of my business, anyway. It sounds so exciting. I sincerely hope you hear from her really soon and that she wants to buy all of your designs. Now that would be really something," Dolores says. "Jackie Kennedy! She's one fabulous lady!"

"Yuh, she sure is."

Dolores taps her mouth with her left index finger. She does not mess up her pink frosty lipstick.

"You know, Abby. I could use a new Christmas dress. Something long, simple yet unusual. A one of a kind. Would you design something for me? I'm pretty handy with a sewing machine and could make a pattern from your sketches."

"Are you kidding? I'd love to!"

"Do you think you could have it ready by the end of this month?"

"You bet! I work fast. The second you asked me two seconds ago, ideas started floating around in my head."

"Then it's a deal," Dolores says.

She extends her hand and we shake on it.

"Let me pay you now for your services so you can add it to your Barbie doll fund," she says.

"Oh no, I wouldn't dream of charging you. This will be a present from me to you. On the house. An exclusive design from Abilea Coutures."

"Why, thank you, Abby. That's very generous of you, but you'll never earn enough for a Barbie doll by doing business this way."

"Don't worry about me," I say. "My piggy bank's getting full. Anna Maria's Nonna Adelaide has been a regular customer."

"I see. So, if you won't take any money for your talents, how about I pay you a dollar to wipe down the bar and wash our two glasses in the sink?"

"That seems like a lot of money for something that'll take no time. I don't even charge that much for my design work," I say.

"Work is work," Dolores says.

"Well, okay. And as Auntie Rina always says, 'Never look a gift horse in the mouth.' "

Dumb, Abby, dumb. And I was doing such a good job of keeping Auntie Rina's name out of the conversation. Dolores is quiet as she pays me the dollar for the cleanup. "You know, Abby, I understand that your family might be worried about my relationship with Max. After all, he's been a bachelor for so long and is set in his ways," Dolores says. "But I want you to know that I love your uncle very, very much."

Dolores holds up her right hand. Her middle finger and index finger are stuck together like she's doing scout's honor.

"Me and Max are like two peas in a pod," she says, "even though there is a little bit of an age difference between us."

I can't do the exact arithmetic that quickly in my head, but

Uncle Max is at least twenty years older than Dolores. That's more than a little bit of an age difference.

"Do you think Uncle Max will pop the question?" I ask.

"We've talked about a future together," Dolores says. "We'll see. Who knows? Maybe Santa will bring me a ring for Christmas."

"I hope so. Don't worry, I'll make your Christmas dress a knockout. Then Uncle Max will propose to you."

"Thank you, Abby," she says, and leans over to give me a kiss on the cheek.

I really mean what I just said to Dolores. But I am just a bit worried about how Auntie Rina will take the news if they get engaged. The office door opens and Uncle Max comes out with Sy.

"Let's go," Uncle Max says. "If I don't get Abby home by a reasonable hour, Betty and Rina will send out the mounted police."

"Where should we go?" Dolores asks.

"I'm thinking the Fish Shanty," Uncle Max answers. "Some steamed lobsters and crab salad sound perfect."

"Wait, Max," Dolores says. Then she leans over to say something to him softly, without actually whispering in his ear, which would appear rude.

"Abby," Uncle Max says. "Dolores is concerned about you eating nonkosher food, especially shellfish."

Our kitchen at home is kosher. We have separate dishes and silverware and cooking stuff for meat and dairy. Mummy never buys meat in the supermarket, only from Sam, the kosher butcher, who delivers in his truck from Boston every Wednesday night around seven o'clock.

"Lobster and crab are shellfish, right?" I ask.

"Yes," Uncle Max says.

"And is shrimp shellfish, too?" I ask.

"Yes," Uncle Max answers again.

"And shrimp is in Chinese egg rolls?"

"Yes."

"Well, I've had shrimp lots of times then, and I like it a lot. So I guess I'll like lobster and crab just fine."

"Don't tell me your Auntie Rina has given up the dietary laws?" Uncle Max asks.

"Oh no. We're kosher superstrict for both the upstairs and the downstairs kitchens. But Auntie Rina decided it would be okay to get Chinese food takeout from the Cathay House and we eat it on the porch table with paper plates and plastic forks. That way we're not actually breaking the kosher rules inside the house. Auntie Rina really loves those Chinese spareribs and egg rolls."

Uncle Max shakes his head from side to side. Then he turns to face Dolores.

"That's typical of my sister," he says. "She tells everybody else to follow her rules, but when it comes to herself, it's a different story."

My face droops and my stomach flip-flops. I made another mistake. I ratted out Auntie Rina. If Mummy were here, she'd yell at me and say I was airing my dirty laundry in public, which is something you're never supposed to do. I'm a traitor, a regular Benedict Arnold.

Sy takes us down in the elevator and Dolores sits with me in the big backseat of the DeSoto Firedome. It's chilly. The temperature dropped in the time we were in the Pink Elephant. Maybe the television meteorologist is right about a frost tonight.

Meeting Dolores was exciting. Going to the Fish Shanty will be exciting. But as I press my face against the cold car window I feel sad. I've collected too many secrets. I've got the secret about what's in the letters to Jackie. I've got the secret about messing up the witches' house. I've got the secret about losing Mei. I've got the secret about Uncle Max and Dolores's maybe engagement. And I've got the secret of Uncle Max, Dolores, and Sy knowing that we eat Chinese food with pork and shrimp, which is *treyf*.

All of those secrets feel heavy. But the heaviest secret of them all is what I did to one of the witch ladies. I know she got hit in the face when I tossed those last two rotten eggs over my shoulder. She made a noise like it hurt. Why did I do that? Maybe Mei got lost as punishment for what I did. Maybe one of the witches gave me the evil eye. But then again, I could have lost Mei before the mission if a trick-or-treater from another neighborhood gave me the evil eye. I don't know. Maybe somebody out there is still giving me the evil eye. It's probably too late, but what the heck, it can't hurt. When nobody in the DeSoto Firedome is looking at me, I turn my head over my left shoulder and say "*keynehore*... poo poo poo," and make three quick little tongue thrusts.

12

You Can't Pull the Wool Over Effie's Eyes

"Abby, you mind telling me what's going on?"

Effie is in the kitchen making us a snack. She pours herself a cup of tea and me a glass of grape juice. Then she opens a new box of Hydrox™ chocolate sandwich cookies and dumps a pile on a plate. Mummy buys them instead of Oreos™ because they are kosher and Oreos are not.

"What do you mean?" I ask.

Effie is the tallest woman I've ever met. She stands six feet or more in her stockings. She's our housekeeper and cleans the downstairs on Tuesdays and the upstairs on Fridays. She's been with us forever.

"I know this house like the back of my hand. I know where everything belongs, so when something's missing, I know that, too," Effie says. "Where's your cute little rag doll? She hasn't been on your shelf for a few weeks now."

I slink down in my chair.

"She's gone."

"How did that happen?" Effie asks.

"I took her out with me trick-or-treating and I lost her."

Effie sets her teacup back on its saucer. She looks at me but says nothing.

"Are you going to yell at me?" I say.

"That's not my job. I know you like to keep her in your pocket when you wear those pajamas in the house, but I can't understand for the life of me why you'd take your favorite doll that came all the way from China out on Halloween night."

Now it's my turn to say nothing.

"Does your Mama or Auntie Rina know about any of this?"

I shake my head. "I didn't tell them. I've been hoping she'll turn up."

"Uh-huh," Effie says.

"Please don't tell them," I say.

"That's not my place, either," Effie says. "But you can't keep it from them forever. Pretty soon they'll realize that the doll is missing, and that's when the questions will start coming."

"Effie, how long have you known me?" I ask.

"Since you were brand spanking new," she says.

"Do you remember a baby picture of me with a pink ribbon in my hair?"

"Sure. The lady across the street's husband took that picture. The one whose husband was a cop. That was sad what happened to him."

"Mrs. Whelan," I say.

"She bought a cute picture frame for it, too, I remember. Your mama kept it in the nursery."

"Really!"

"Right up on top of the bureau," Effie says.

"Gee, that's really funny because when I asked Mummy about it, she said there never was a picture."

Effie turns her back to me and runs the dishwater.

"Maybe I got my houses mixed up," Effie says. "Maybe the baby picture was in the other house I clean."

Her back is still turned to me.

Mrs. Whelan might have a problem with the bottle but, *far-shtunkene* drunk or not, I believe her. If you're going to make up a crazy story, why do it about a baby picture? I'm no expert, but I'm positive Mrs. Whelan was sober when she told me. And if she was sober, then what's so important about a baby picture that it's making Mummy and Effie lie?

"Sure, Effie, sure. If you say so."

13

What Gives, Jackie?

ABIGAIL LEAH SHAPIRO

November 17, 1959

Dear Jackie,

I suppose you know that it is now November. I get it that I didn't give you enough time to answer me when I sent those first and second letters together. But it's November. Almost a whole month has passed—more than enough time for you to answer me, don't you think? Please do your best to answer all three of my letters in just one letter by Thanksgiving. Okay? I'd appreciate it very much.

Speaking of Thanksgiving, it's my favorite American holiday. I'm not crazy about turkey, but I love stuffing and pie. That's because I stuff myself with pie. Ha-ha-ha, just a little joke. My old favorite pie was squash pie, but now my new favorite is apple. I asked Mummy if we could also

have blueberry pie this year. She looked
at me like I had two heads. She's been
supercranky lately, so I've been staying out
of her hair. No, that's not the truth. She's
always supercranky, not just lately. But the
staying out of her hair part is the truth.

My brother, Marty, doesn't like pie. He
just likes to shake up the can of whipped
cream and shoot it into his mouth. Believe
you me, Marty has a big mouth, too. It's
like a giant bat cave in there. Then when
his mouth is all filled up, he lets some
dribble out and he chases me around the
house saying, "mad dog, mad dog." My brother,
Marty, is so funny. But I'm thinking
I don't want him to do the whipped
cream thing this year. It's on account of
something bad I did with a can of shaving
cream. I'm sorry, I can't tell you, I pinky-
promised Marty and his friends Todd and
Harry. As long as I'm being extrahonest
with you, I'll say that the thing with
Marty isn't my only secret. I've got other
secrets, and it's getting to be hard work
keeping them. One of them has to do with
my Uncle Max. I don't think I told you
about him yet. On second thought, maybe I
shouldn't tell you anything private about
him. He doesn't walk the straight and
narrow, if you know what I mean. I wouldn't
want Senator Kennedy to report him to
the FBI. All I'll say about his secret
is that I don't think he's going to be a

89

bachelor for much longer, only nobody in my family knows about it.

It's time for fashion talk! Here's another fabulous design from Abilea Coutures. I figure you must go to a lot of parties or give a lot of parties. Am I right on that one? This one-piece dress is silky and has a zebra pattern. I may have gotten the idea from the black-and-white-striped bathing suit that Barbie wears. I do not have my Barbie yet. I am just saying that as a news flash item, not for any other reason, like to make you feel guilty for not answering my letters and paying me for my designs. Because I now have two dollars and sixty-five cents saved in my piggy bank, so it won't be long now before I get my Barbie. So please don't feel like you have to buy my stuff so I can buy a Barbie. I'm doing okay on my own. I just would like to hear from you one of these moons. I would like to have your honest opinion about my fashion designs. I mean, what gives, Jackie?

Bye!
Your Friend in Fashion,
Abby Shapiro

P.S. Like I said, I really don't need your money anymore, but if you do want to keep all of the designs so far and pay for them, your account is up to sixty-five cents. But that's entirely up to you.

P.P.S. Here's why I gave you gloves for your party dress. I notice in all the magazine pictures of you that you wear them a lot. So you must like them. That's one thing we do not have in common. I don't care if Mummy and Auntie Rina always tell me that a lady never goes anywhere without her gloves. Me personally, I hate their guts-not Mummy and Auntie Rina-the gloves. Mummy makes me wear these white, stubby cotton gloves whenever I get all dressed up for a special party, like Marty's Bar Mitzvah or for synagogue on the High Holy Days. But I always go into the ladies' room and ditch them in the wastebasket. Then I tell Mummy that when I washed and dried my hands, somebody must have taken them by mistake. Once I ran outside during the service and pitched them down a drain sewer. Mummy never suspected a thing.

P.P.P.S. Did you ever lose something that was so important that it made your heart feel like it was cracking like frozen taffy smashed against the kitchen counter? That happened to me. It's been almost three weeks since I lost my most special doll, Mei. She came to me all the way from China. It happened on Halloween when that something else happened that I can't talk about, because I'd be a rat. I'm just glad that Mummy hasn't noticed that Mei is missing from her spot on my doll shelves. She wouldn't feel badly for me. She'd just yell and remind me how I am always so careless. I look for Mei every single day after school. I say little prayers that I'll find her, but I have a feeling that's never going to happen. I gotta go now, Jackie. A big fat tear is about to splash on your letter.

14
Buried Treasure

"Abby, I'm going to lie down for a while," Mummy says. "I have a splitting headache."

"Ever heard of privacy?" I ask.

I need a Do Not Disturb sign to tack up on the Pink Palace door. Mummy has a rude habit of barging in without knocking first. It's a good thing I just finished the final touches for Dolores's dress design. If she had startled me two seconds earlier, I might have messed up the trim and would have had to start the sketch over from scratch. Forget Do Not Disturb, I think Fashion Designer at Work might be a better idea.

"Go down to the cedar closet and try on your sweaters from last year," Mummy says. "Separate the ones you've outgrown so I can give them to Effie for her nieces."

I go downstairs to the basement and into the cedar closet. Forget it! What does Mummy think I am, a giant? The sweaters are in a see-through bag on the highest shelf. There's no way I can reach it, even if I stand up on tippy-toes.

"Who's there?" Marty calls out.

"The Lone Ranger," I say.

I gallop from the cedar closet into Marty's laboratory. Marty is hunched over his microscope wearing a white lab coat.

"A fiery horse with the speed of light, a cloud of dust, and a hearty Hi-yo, Silver. Away!" I announce.

"Quit it, Abby!" Marty says in a voice that does not please me at all.

"You don't have to be so snippety-snappety with me," I tell my brother. "Everyone else in this house is always in a permanently crummy mood. You don't have to be that way, too."

"Sorry," he says.

I am not convinced that he means it.

"It's just that I need to concentrate when I use the microscope," Marty explains. "This lab report is due on Monday."

"Yuh, okay, fine."

Marty's science laboratory is the basement bathroom, which isn't much of a bathroom. It's really just a toilet room.

"What are you doing down here, anyway?" Marty asks.

He doesn't look up from the microscope when he talks to me. He's also not wearing his glasses. He can't wear them and look through the microscope at the same time.

"I gotta try on some clothes, and they're too high up for me to reach."

"Why don't you ask Mummy to help?"

"She's napping."

"Hold on. I'll be done with this soon."

I sit on the old toilet to wait. The cover is missing, and the cracked seat wobbles. The flush doesn't work properly, so the water runs constantly and sounds like there is a river flowing underneath my *tush*. There's no sink, no mirror, no window, and no cabinets in the toilet room. There's just one countertop, which is big enough to hold all of Marty's science stuff. He has a microscope, glass slides, tweezers, and a lot of bottles with skulls and bones across the front of the labels.

It's so boring in here. There's nothing to do except watch

Marty's curved back or look at the poster of the periodic table of elements he tacked up on the wall. If it were the periodic table of elephants, then that would be interesting.

Marty looks up from the microscope every so often, puts his glasses on, and writes in his notebook. At least he's not dissecting a frog. He had to do that at the end of seventh grade. He brought home a frog in a jar filled with liquid. I thought it was just floating or doing the backstroke until Marty unscrewed the jar lid. P U! It smelled just as bad as the sewer beds we pass when we take a ride to get ice cream at the farm stand. Marty explained that the frog was preserved in the same liquid that keeps dead people from going bad. I made up a riddle and tested it out on Susie Applegate.

"What do dead frogs and dead people have in common?" I asked her.

"Ooh, that is so gross," Susie said. "I don't know. What?"

"Formaldehyde!" I said, feeling quite superior and proud of myself.

"What's formaldehyde?" she asked.

So I explained that it was a chemical to preserve dead things.

"My great-uncle Phillip was cremated when he died. They toasted him into ashes, so he never had any of that liquid. And lots of times frogs die when they hop onto the road and a car runs them over or if a snake eats them whole. So not only is your riddle stupid, but it makes absolutely no sense at all."

That made me hate Susie Applegate even more than I already did.

"Marty, are you almost done?" I ask impatiently.

"Just give me one more minute," Marty says.

"Good, because if you stay bent over that microscope for much longer, you'll freeze in that position and look like the Hunchback of Notre Dame for the rest of your life," I warn.

"You sound like Mummy. You want to grow up and be like her? Think for yourself, Abby."

What's up with Marty today? He's dumping on me and Mummy in the same breath. I don't like that. He shouldn't lump me in with her. I'm nothing like Mummy. I'm my own person.

"Yes, sir, Marty, sir."

I lift my right arm and give Marty a full military salute. Only because the toilet room is so tiny, I accidentally bean him in the head.

"Stop it, Abby! Not everything is a game," Marty says.

"I never said it was."

Marty goes back to looking through the microscope.

"Marty?"

"What?"

"When are we all going to do army again? I don't want being a lieutenant to go to waste," I say. "Can we go for a hike or spy on the Connolly kids?"

"At present there are no plans for any more operations," Marty says.

"Oh."

"Marty?"

"Now what?" he says.

"Hanukkah is soon."

"I know."

"Did you get me a gift yet?" I ask. "Because I have a gift for you."

"Not yet. What do you want?"

"I want a bra and Mummy won't get me one. Will you buy one for me?" I ask.

Marty throws his pencil down on the counter.

"That's it!" he shouts. "Stop clinging and hanging on me all the time. And don't ask me to do things like buy you a bra. Jeez, Abby. I'm your brother."

"I'm just kidding, Marty," I say. "Can't you take a joke?"

"Just do girl stuff with your friends and I'll do guy stuff with my friends. We're not little kids anymore. Do you understand that I'm your brother and not your playmate? That's why there'll be no more army operations. At least not with you."

"Fine! No sweat off my back!"

I stare right back at Marty and I think he's a stranger. Everything between us seemed to change right after Operation Whiskey-India-Tango-Charlie-Hotel-Echo-Sierra. His two best friends must have teased him something wicked. That's why I'm kicked out of the army. I bet it was mostly Todd. I should have bitten him even harder when I was little. Now it's like everything I do annoys Marty, but I'm thinking it should be the other way around. I could tell him that I know the truth. I know he used me. He never wanted me to be a true member of his army. Marty just needed an ace pitcher to slither like a snake up the witches' lawn and get the wiffle balls. Yuh, I could say plenty to Marty if I wanted to. But I don't.

"You know what," I say. "I'll get a ladder. I can do it myself. I don't need your help."

"Don't be stupid. You want to break your neck?" he says.

"Now who sounds like Mummy?"

"Just show me what you want me to do," he says as he follows me into the cedar closet.

"Up there. On the way top shelf. That big plastic case with the zipper."

Marty reaches up and pulls down the sweater bag with the help of a wooden hanger. A shoebox tumbles down with it, and photographs scatter all over the floor. We kneel on the floor and scoop them back into a pile.

"Boy, these people look miserable," Marty says. "Nobody's smiling."

"Yuh, I've seen some of these old photographs before. They're all dead relatives from the Old Country. I guess they didn't have too much to smile about over there."

Marty looks at each one, then passes it along to me. There are names and dates on the back of each one. Some of the photographs have a heavy, black cardboard backing. Marty freezes when he comes to a small pocket-sized photograph. He studies it for a few seconds, then flips it over to read what's written on the back.

"Take a look at this," Marty says.

He hands me a photograph of two young women wearing the prettiest sailor dresses I have ever seen. They're smiling and standing in front of a railing on what looks like an ocean boardwalk.

"This one on the left looks like Auntie Rina, only without glasses," I say. "I don't have a clue who this other woman is, but she sure is pretty."

"Read what's on the back," Marty says.

"A perfect day of fun and sailing. Rina and Betty. Cape Cod. August 14, 1924," I say out loud. "Betty? Oh my God, that's Mummy?"

I almost can't breathe. That beautiful young woman in the photo is my mother. Even though the picture is in black and white, you can tell she's wearing lipstick and rouge on her cheeks. Her hair is styled in a permanent wave bob. She looks like a regular movie star.

"Give me the picture. I'll put it back," Marty says.

I take one last look, long and hard, then finally give it back to Marty. He puts all of the photographs into the shoebox and back up on the top shelf.

"Marty?"

"What?"

"Are you ever sorry about what we did to the witches? Doesn't your conscience get to you? Mine bugs me all the time."

"Why are you bringing this up now?" he asks. "What does this have to do with anything?"

"I don't know. It's just that I think about it a lot. I think we shouldn't have done it. I shouldn't have done it. Uncle Max asked me why we didn't just ask them for the balls back. I mean, maybe they were just holding them for us. Maybe they just wanted us to say hello or something or teach us how to say wiffle ball in witch language. I don't know."

"You told Uncle Max what we did?"

Marty says each word with a matching hard poke to my shoulder. I drop the bag of sweaters.

"Ow! No, I just said our wiffle balls were in a pail by their door, that's all. I'd never tell on you. You're my brother."

"Then stop thinking about it," Marty says. "It's over. Got it?"

"Yuh, I got it. But answer me this. If they really stole the wiffle balls, why would they leave them outside in the pail? Huh?"

Marty keeps silent.

"Just what I thought."

Marty picks up my sweaters and carries them to the Pink Palace.

"Put them on my bed," I order.

Marty unzips the bag and takes out a cable-knit skating sweater. He rolls it up into a ball and stuffs it under his shirt to shape a large hump on his back.

"Quatheemoto at your thervith," he says with a lisp, a limp, and a roll of the eyes.

I know he's trying to apologize for being mean. But for the first time in my life, I'm not interested in what my brother has to say, even if it *is* kind of funny. I'm going to give him a dose of his own medicine. Let's see how he likes it.

"Stop it, Marty! Not everything's a game," I say. "Thanks for helping me, but I'm busy now. Leave the sweater on the bed and close the door on your way out."

Marty looks a little taken aback.

I open up my sketchbook to a clean page. There is something

I must draw which is not for Barbie, Jackie, or Dolores. It is for me. I close my eyes for a moment and recall the photograph of Auntie Rina and Mummy in their crisp sailor dresses. I pick up a charcoal pencil and draw them from memory, down to every last, perfect detail.

15

Ho Ho Ho, Merry Christmas to All, and Tough Toenails to Mummy

I'm in the Pink Palace, sitting at my desk counting my Barbie doll fund money. I lose my place twice listening to their fighting.

"Hank, for the love of Pete, turn down that blasted hi-fi!" Mummy shouts from the living room.

This is the second time she asks my father to turn down the music. But each time the volume goes way up, like it's broadcasting a PA system through the house. I'm sure Auntie Rina and Uncle Morris hear every word of "When the Saints Go Marching In" loud and clear all the way upstairs.

"Don't you dare touch that switch!" my father yells.

"Too late," she yells back. The hi-fi stops playing music.

My father swears at her and stomps downstairs to the basement. There's an old television set down there with rabbit ears that are broken, so the picture is always woozy. He turns up the volume twice as loud as the hi-fi. I wait a few minutes before I open my bedroom door to peek outside. The living room lights are still on, so I know Mummy is sitting on the sofa reading the newspaper. I want to talk to her. I will give her one last chance to buy me a bra.

"Hi, Mum," I say. "Do you mind if I keep you company?"

"Of course not," she says with a sigh. "But I'd like to finish reading the newspaper."

"I'll be quiet," I say.

"Good," she says, "because I could use some of that right now."

I sit down at the other end of the sofa. Her feet are propped up on the middle cushion. Her toes poke through holes in her stockings. The bottoms of her feet don't look clean. I look away because when I see that stuff about my mother, my stomach hurts, and I get sad first, and then so angry that I just want to punch her.

While I wait for her to finish the newspaper I pull out of my dungaree pockets the angels I made after school at Anna Maria's house. I love going to the Tuccis' house at Christmastime. The tree looks so pretty all decorated, and Nonna Adelaide bakes a million cookies with candy in the middle and sprinkles on top. It's always happy at the Tuccis' house. Anna Maria had four boxes of tissues for us to make angels. She decorates her family's Christmas presents with them. Mine didn't look so much like angels. They looked more like all-white finger puppets or Casper the Friendly Ghost.

Mummy finally folds the section of the newspaper and looks at me over her reading glasses. The half lenses are greasy with fingerprints all over them.

"What are those things?" she asks.

"Angel dolls. I made them at Anna Maria's."

"Throw them away," she yells.

"Why? What's the big deal?"

"The big deal is that they're Christmas decorations, that's what they are! It's a sin for you to play with them in this house. *Bubbie* Lena would never approve. And neither would Auntie Rina, for that matter. She would tell you just like I am to get rid of them."

Mummy goes all shaky, like someone plugged her into an electric socket.

"Don't have a cow! And would you quit it already with *Bubbie* Lena? Stop dragging her into every conversation!"

"Your *Bubbie* Lena, of blessed memory, was a religious woman who taught us the right way to conduct our lives. So don't start wanting to be like people you're not. And don't disrespect Auntie Rina's wishes, either."

"You never make any sense. Ever! And neither did *Bubbie* Lena. She didn't even know my name."

"I've had it with you, Abby," Mummy shouts.

"I've had it with you, too. But getting back to the angels, they are just angels. Everybody believes in angels. Rabbi Levine talks about angels in Bible stories at Sunday school. And another thing, since Auntie Rina isn't sitting here with us on the sofa, I have no way of knowing what her wishes really are. She might like my angels and say they look like dolls. I think I'll run upstairs and ask her."

"Just throw them out. Now!"

"I don't think so," I say as I stuff the angels back into my dungaree pockets. "What's next, that I can't be best friends with Anna Maria, because she's not Jewish? Is that what you're working up to? Because I bet that's what's in your crazy head."

Mummy throws the newspaper on the floor. "How dare you say that to me! This family loves Anna Maria just the same as her family loves you. I simply forbid you to bring outside things into this house that do not have a place here. Have I made myself clear, Abby? I hope so, because I am sick and tired of your nonsense."

"My nonsense?" I shout at her. "You're nothing but a big phony, that's what you are. When you were making breakfast yesterday, I heard you singing along to 'White Christmas' on the radio. What was that all about? Huh, huh?"

"That's different," she says. "Bing Crosby was singing, and I love anything he sings. I'm a fan. It's not like I was singing a Christmas song."

"Well I like 'O Come All Ye Faithful,'" I say. "I think it's a beautiful melody, so I'm a fan of whoever wrote that carol."

I belt out the first few lines through "O come ye, O come ye, to Bethlehem." I cup my hands together like I'm praying.

"Stop it, Abby. Stop testing me!" Mummy shrieks. "You never give me one moment of peace!"

I get up from the sofa and start toward the Pink Palace. But I will not let her have the last word.

"You're a terrible mother. You don't care about me. You don't care if everybody in school makes fun of me."

"Now what are you talking about?" Mummy sighs her deepest, most exasperating sigh. "Who makes fun of you?"

"Susie Applegate and a bunch of girls were laughing at me behind my back. They said it looked like I had cupcakes under my sweater. I need a bra and I want one for Hanukkah. It falls under the category of clothes, stuff that I need. And stuff that I need is legally allowed for Hanukkah, so it won't be breaking another one of your stupid rules."

I keep to myself that Susie really said cherries, not cupcakes.

"Go to your room, Abby!" Mummy yells. "Right this very moment!"

"Sure thing," I yell back. "It'll be my pleasure. Anything to get away from you!"

I take my time, walking slowly from the living room to the Pink Palace. And while I do, I sing on the top of my lungs the rest of "O Come All Ye Faithful."

16
Giddyup, Jackie

ABIGAIL LEAH SHAPIRO

December 20, 1959

Dear Jackie,

I hope you have a jolly holly Merry Christmas with Senator Kennedy and your little girl, Caroline. I think Christmas is great because people are so friendly to each other. Even if they hate each other during the rest of the year, they're nice during the Christmas season. I just realized that if I celebrated Christmas, I'd have to be nice to Susie Applegate. It would only be for the month of December, but even for that short a time, I still don't know if I could do it. Maybe it's a good thing that I don't celebrate Christmas.

Jackie, when your daughter Caroline gets older and if she has some friends who celebrate Hanukkah, would you get upset if she played the dreidel game with them?

Or what if she learned some Hanukkah songs and liked singing them because they were catchy tunes? Or how about if she ate potato latkes with apple sauce or sour cream or both those toppings mixed together? Would you tell your daughter that if she did stuff from her friends' religion, then she wouldn't like her own anymore? Of course you'd never say that, because it's dumb. I knew you'd feel that way. Thanks!

Anyway, I have a Christmas surprise for you! It's a new outfit for you to wear for your hobby of horseback riding. My favorite parts of the outfit are the pockets. They look so cute with the triangles. I know you ride horses because I saw a picture of you doing just that in one of the magazines. I've never ridden a horse, but I bet it's lots of fun. If I rode a horse, I'd pretend I was a cowgirl like Annie Oakley and be a sharpshooter in Buffalo Bill's Wild West show. Jackie, be careful when you ride. Auntie Rina knows somebody who was thrown from a horse and then they had to have their spleen removed. I'm not really sure what a spleen is or what it does.

Bye!
Your Friend in Fashion,
Abby

P.S. I wiped clean your charge account bill. You don't owe me any money if you ever get around to reading my letters and deciding to keep the designs. I've got enough saved for a Barbie doll, and my name is on a list at the toy store for when they come in next week.

P.P.S. MERRY CHRISTMAS!

P.P.P.S. My hobby is collecting foreign dolls. Did I tell you that already?

17

Another Secret

It's so cold outside, my nose hair is frozen stiff. When I wiggle my nose, it feels like bristles from a whisk broom are sweeping the insides of my nostrils.

Auntie Rina swears it's going to snow tonight. She can tell without watching the weatherman on the television or looking at the sky. She knows it's going to snow when the bunion on her right foot throbs like crazy. If she's correct, that'll mean 1959 will be one for the record books. Everyone will have a white Christmas Eve and a white first night of Hanukkah, too. This year the two holidays fall on the same calendar date. I think that's really nice. People can be happy and celebrate together and not think about the stuff that makes them different.

It might be freezing outside, but the money from my piggy bank is burning a hole in my coat pocket. This is the second time I've walked the whole length of Main Street, up and down on both sides of the street. The sidewalks are packed wall-to-wall with last-minute shoppers. Everyone's arms are full with shopping bags containing gift-wrapped packages with big red bows, plastic sprigs of holly, and tree ornaments.

I earned an extra two dollars the last two Saturdays helping Auntie Rina with the gift wrapping in our store. We go all out at Christmas with three kinds of ribbon and little silver bells, sprigs of plastic holly, or real candy canes. The customers can chose which decorations they want. We were so mobbed with shoppers that Auntie Rina had to call in the battalions. That's what she calls Flo, Kathleen, and Mary, our part-time salesgirls. The store will stay open until six o'clock tonight for any last-minute stragglers. That means husbands who save their shopping until the last possible minute.

If I don't make a decision soon, I'm going to turn into a human popsicle. I've been standing in front of Mayfair's for the last ten minutes.

"Excuse me, hon, can I help you?"

A lady with gray hair and a tape measure draped around her neck like a doctor's stethoscope pops her head outside the door to Mayfair's. The rest of her body remains inside the store.

"I'm just waiting," I say.

"Brrr. It's so cold," she says, wrapping her arms around herself behind the glass. "Why don't you come inside? We've got hot cocoa," she says in a singsong voice, like that'll do the trick to lure me inside. "Santa will be very upset and think you're naughty when he comes down your chimney and finds that you've caught a death of a cold on Christmas eve."

This woman is loony. I am loitering in front of an undergarments store. Would a girl who needs a bra still believe in Santa Claus?

"I'm okay," I tell her.

"But if you change your mind, don't be shy."

I say thanks and wave and move down one store so she can't spy on me through the window. The truth is, I'm not waiting for anybody. I've been standing outside Mayfair's because I don't know what to do. I know I have enough to buy a Barbie like planned. But I don't know if a bra costs one dollar and eighty-four cents, which is what I'll have left over if I buy the Barbie, or if a bra costs more than four dollars and eighty-four cents, which is all I have to my name. I don't think I can afford to buy both, so all I have to do is waltz into Mayfair's and ask how much a training bra costs. I thought it would be so easy, no problem. Just go and be a grownup and show Mummy I didn't need her. But I can't make my feet walk through the door. And if I don't come back to the store with a Barbie doll, what will I tell Mummy and Auntie Rina? Peterson's Toy and Hobby will only hold the doll until five o'clock. It's four o'clock now and I'm hopelessly stuck. I really don't know if I'm a woman who needs a bra or a little girl who needs a doll.

A car horn toots, and it startles me. I spin around.

"Abby!"

The Desoto Firedome pulls over to the curb. Dolores waves to me through the open rear window. I go over to the car and peek inside. It's just her, with Sy driving. The car is filled with wrapped packages.

"What are you doing here all by your lonesome?" Dolores asks.

"Just stuff. Hey, where's Uncle Max?" I ask.

"At the Pink Elephant, as usual," Dolores says. "You should come by. The place looks grand. We're getting ready for our New Year's Eve opening."

"Well, good luck," I say as I walk away.

"Abby, wait!" Dolores shouts.

She opens the car door and gets out. She's walking toward me wearing a brown suede coat with mink trim on the collar and cuffs. Her boots are brown suede, too, with very high spike heels. Dolores looks like a model on the runway if a fashion show runway were outdoors on Main Street on the coldest day of the year.

Dolores grabs my hand. She's not wearing gloves and there's no diamond ring on her finger. Not yet, anyway.

"What's going on?" she asks.

The cold air finally gets to me big-time. I shiver from head to toe.

"Get in the car," Dolores says.

I shake my head.

"I can't."

"Sy," she yells, "come back for me in thirty minutes, okay?"

Sy drives off, and Dolores pulls me into her arms to warm me up.

"Talk to me, Abby. Tell me what's wrong," she says.

"Everything," I say. "Everything's wrong."

Dolores looks up at the big picture window at Bowie's pet store. Puppies are climbing all over each other and nipping their litter mates' tails.

"You weren't really planning to go into the pet store, were you?" she asks.

I shake my head no.

"I didn't think so," she says. "Come on. I'll take you into Mayfair's. That's where you want to go, isn't it?"

"Yes," I whisper.

Dolores doesn't say a word as she grabs my arm. She leads me inside the store. The same lady with the gray hair and tape measure greets us.

"Oh, there you are! Your daughter was waiting for you for the longest time," she says to Dolores.

The saleslady's tone is sarcastic, like Dolores is a bad mother for making me wait out in the cold.

"Well, I'm here now," Dolores says.

We hang our coats on the hooks outside a changing room. Then the saleslady pulls aside the curtain, steps inside with us, and draws the curtain closed.

"All right, deary," she says, "you'll need to take off your sweater. I can't see what you've got sprouting with your top on."

"You know what," Dolores says, "I'll do the fitting. Just leave the tape measure with me."

"That's not how we do things here at Mayfair's," she says. "We're highly professional."

"Well, that's how we're going to do it today, if you don't mind,"

Dolores says, helping herself to the tape measure from the saleslady's neck.

She slides open the changing room curtain and gestures for the saleslady to leave. Then Dolores closes the curtain and whispers in my ear, "We showed her. Some *yenta*, huh!"

"You know Yiddish?" I ask.

"Oh, I've picked up a few words here and there."

Dolores measures me above and below my bosoms, all the while singing "It's Beginning to Look a Lot Like Christmas." I know she does that not just because she's full of Christmas cheer. She sings to relax me. It works.

"Don't go anywhere now, you hear!"

I giggle. I know it's a joke because I'm half-undressed. Dolores returns to the changing room a few minutes later with several different styles of training bras.

"For the life of me," she says, "I don't know why they call them training bras. It sounds so silly, like you're in the military."

I smile. That's something I would say. I slip on the first model. There's really no formed cup, just stretchy stuff to hold me in place. Dolores adjusts the straps on my shoulders.

"Well, what do you think?" she asks, patting my back.

I nod. I do not want to look at myself in the full-length mirror wearing the training bra just yet. I don't have to. It feels just right, like it was meant for me.

"Abby, do you want to try on any of the other styles, just to compare?" Dolores asks.

"No. I'm happy with this one," I tell her.

"Well, that was easy enough. You don't have to take it off. Just get dressed while I take care of it," Dolores says as she pulls off the price ticket from the back of the bra.

I sit on the bench in the changing room and I know I should feel happy, but I'm not. I start to cry.

"What's all this?" Dolores asks when she returns. She's holding a Mayfair's bag.

"I don't know," I say. "Half the time I don't know how I feel or how I'm supposed to feel. Mummy says I'm as moody as all outdoors."

Dolores hands me a tissue from her purse and sits next to me on the bench.

"Dry your tears," she says. "Today is an important day in your life. You're becoming a woman. There's no need to be sad. Your body is getting ready for the next set of changes."

I know what she's talking about. I know about it because the girls at school talk about it. They know because their mothers gave them booklets about it. But not mine.

"I wish Mummy was more like you," I say.

"Talk to her. Tell her how you feel. And make sure to tell her that I bought you a bra and a spare," Dolores says, lifting the Mayfair's bag in her hand. "I don't want any bad feelings between me and your family."

"Can I pay you back for the bras?" I ask.

"Absolutely not," she says. "After all, you're my personal fashion designer. Wait until you see how the dress fits. Perfect, like a kidskin glove. I told your Uncle Max to make sure he has plenty of film in the camera so when I wear it tomorrow for Christmas dinner, he can take lots of pictures for you to put in your professional portfolio."

I hug Dolores tight around the middle. I don't want to let go.

"Well, Sy should be waiting for me, so I have to leave. But you have a wonderful first night of Hanukkah," Dolores says. "We'll see each other soon, Abby. I promise. And I'll make sure you'll get those photographs, okay?"

"Merry Christmas, Dolores," I say.

She kisses me on the forehead.

"Happy Hanukkah, Abby," she says. "There's a card in the mail with some Hanukkah *gelt* for you and Marty."

I smile. Dolores knows lots of Yiddish words. She said *gelt* instead of "money."

"Thank you for everything."

"No need for thanks, doll," she says as she walks out of the dressing room.

"Dolores, wait!"

She pulls open the curtain just wide enough to talk.

"I hope that you'll be my Aunt Dolores very soon," I say.

"Me too, sweetheart," she says. "Me too."

I leave Mayfair's and run out to Main Street and into the cold. It feels good to run wearing a bra. I look toward the public library and at the big clock. It's a quarter to five. That leaves me fifteen minutes to go to Peterson's Toy and Hobby to pick up my Barbie and then another hour to concoct a story about why I have returned with two new bras.

18
Happy New Year!

"Today was a very interesting day," Uncle Morris says at the supper table.

It's Saturday night and the second day in the new decade. We're eating franks and beans for supper. Mummy grilled the big fat ones called specials.

"I'll say," Auntie Rina agrees. "It was an interesting and exciting day."

"Why?" I ask in between bites.

My hot dog is so huge, it's falling out of the regular-sized bun. Mummy always says somebody would make a killing if they baked giant-sized rolls.

"Well, for one thing, Senator John Fitzgerald Kennedy announced his candidacy for the presidency of the United States today. The waiting is finally over. Now the fun begins," Uncle Morris says.

"He did? I didn't know that. I guess I didn't see it on television today," I say.

I am a little disappointed. Was Jackie there when Senator Kennedy made his announcement? Would I have seen her on television? I wonder what she was wearing.

"Yowzah," Uncle Morris says. "He made his announcement in the Senate caucus room. It was a full press conference."

"I'm very pleased," Auntie Rina says.

"He has been a good senator, right?" I ask.

"Absolutely."

Uncle Morris nods. "He's got lots of integrity. I say if he works as hard for the country as he has for the state of Massachusetts, he'll make a fine president."

"They say a lot of people won't vote for him, because he's a Catholic," Auntie Rina says.

"Why's that?" I ask.

"Just because we've never had a Catholic president before."

"What! That's really stupid," I say. "What's that got to do with him being a good president?"

"Nothing," Auntie Rina says. "That's just foolish talk. People can be ignorant. They're just afraid of something that they don't know or understand. That's the definition of prejudice."

"Mummy's prejudiced," I say.

"I most certainly am not," she says.

"Yes, you are. You're afraid of anything that isn't Jewish."

"*Noch a mol.* 'Here we go again,'" she says. "I am not prejudiced at all. I just want you to understand the importance of your heritage."

"How can I forget when you remind me every two seconds?" I say.

"That's enough," Auntie Rina says.

"Marty, do you discuss Senator Kennedy in your civics class?" Uncle Morris asks.

"Sometimes," Marty answers.

"And what's your opinion about the situation?"

Marty shrugs.

This is how it's been for months. Marty spends most of his time in his bedroom or over at his friends' houses. He doesn't want to hang out with me at all or participate in any dinner conversation.

"I want the beans," my father says.

Wow! My father actually spoke at the dinner table. Usually there's only a grunt and a point.

Auntie Rina sends them down to my brother, who passes to my mother, who passes to my father.

"Then, of course, there was the other big news today, which is kind of related to the first bit of news," Auntie Rina says.

"Yowzah, yowzah," Uncle Morris says.

"Go on, spill," I say. "I'm all ears."

Uncle Morris wipes his mouth and lays his napkin down on his lap. "Well, I was drinking my coffee this morning in the office and going through some invoices when the telephone rang. I don't as a rule pick up the phone. Usually, I let Auntie Rina or your mother do that up front, but today, for some reason, I decided to pick it up. I don't know why, I just did. There was a woman on the other end. She said she had some questions about the types of shoes we carry and in what sizes."

I take a big gulp of my root beer tonic. Uncle Morris isn't telling me anything out of the ordinary, so I don't get what's the big deal here.

"So this woman on the telephone wants to know if we have any stock in a ten and a half or an eleven, but get this," Uncle Morris says, "with a double A width."

"Phew," I whistle. "Those are some big, thin feet."

Having grown up in the shoe biz, I know that a woman with that size foot is not an easy fit. I also know that a woman wearing that size shoe is tall and probably would not be looking for spikes with a skinny high heel.

"You ain't just whistling Dixie," Uncle Morris says. "I told the woman on the phone that we had a few pair of leather flats in stock in that size. To tell you the truth, I think they've been in inventory since before the flood."

"What flood?"

"That just means since the year one," Auntie Rina says.

"What's with you people today? Can't you stop talking in riddles?" I say.

"It means that the shoes have been in stock forever," Auntie Rina says. "We don't have regular customers with that shoe size."

"Oh. Why didn't you just say so?"

"Morris, let me finish the story. At the rate you're telling it, we'll be here until breakfast," Auntie Rina says.

Uncle Morris looks a little sad. I think Auntie Rina burst his bubble.

"So, to make a long story short, guess who wanted the shoes?"

"I don't know, Auntie Rina. Tell me."

"Take a guess. Just one little guess," she says.

Auntie Rina's eyes are all crinkled up, and she only does that when she's laughing really hard or if she's very happy or when she's busting a gut to spill some good news.

"Is it someone I know?"

"Not exactly. Not directly, but you certainly know who she is."

"Is she someone famous?"

"Yes," Auntie Rina says.

"Like movie-star famous?"

"Yes."

"Who, who, who?" I ask.

"You sound like an owl. Take one more guess."

"Is it—"

I am about to say Hayley Mills because I can't wait to see her new movie *Pollyanna*, but my father interrupts.

"For cripe's sakes, already. It was Jackie Kennedy."

I'm angry. Really, really blood-boiling angry. I stare at him, and for the first time in my life, I think he actually makes eye contact with me.

"Oh, Hank," my mother says, "why did you have to go and ruin Abby's fun?"

He doesn't answer. It suits him now to go back to eating. Uncle Morris quietly picks up the pieces and just finishes the story as though there never was this interruption. That's what my family does. They ignore all the bad things. Like when Uncle Max called the day after Christmas to tell the family that he and Dolores got engaged. Auntie Rina blew a gasket and said she didn't want to discuss the matter ever again. And then when the invitation came for the grand opening of the supper club, she just tossed it in the wastebasket.

"Well, Abby, the woman on the telephone was Jackie Kennedy's secretary. She'd heard about our store. She said we had a reputation for carrying very fashionable merchandise," Uncle Morris says.

"It goes to show you that news travels fast in the Bay State," Auntie Rina says.

It takes a few seconds for this to sink into my brain. Then it hits like a tidal wave. I bounce up and down in my seat, and my hands flail up and down and sideways.

"Oh my God, she got the letters, didn't she? Huh? Huh? Her secretary called to give me a message, right? She liked my designs, right? She needed shoes to go with my designs, right? She wants me to design clothes for her, right?"

"Abby, I don't know what you're talking about," Auntie Rina says. "What letters to Jackie Kennedy?"

"This is a sign, one of those *bashert*, 'meant-to-be,' things you're always talking about. Only it's not about falling in love. Don't you all get it? You got a call at the store for shoes for Jackie on the exact day Senator Kennedy announces he's going to run for president."

"Abby, I still don't understand what you're talking about," Auntie Rina says.

"Oh, I've been writing to her, Jackie, since October and showing her my sketches. It's because I had this plan and I...," then I realize I better be careful about what falls out of my mouth, since I lied to Mummy in the first place. "I chose her as a pen pal for a school project. I've been patiently waiting to hear from her. I sent her designs and told her I wanted to be a fashion designer when I grow up."

"Betty, did you know about this?" Auntie Rina asks.

"What?"

"Abby's letters to Jackie Kennedy. Did you know about them?"

"Oh, sure," Mummy says.

"I bet you got the call for shoes because Jackie loves my clothes. I just know it. I bet I'll get a personal phone call from her soon. I'm so excited. When is she coming into the store to pick up the shoes?"

"She's not," Uncle Morris says. "Her secretary just asked that they be mailed to Senator Kennedy's Massachusetts office. They already went out in the late afternoon mail."

"Oh," I say.

I can't hide my disappointment. That makes me think that I should have addressed Jackie's letters to the Massachusetts office, and not to the one in Washington, DC.

"The secretary didn't mention anything about your letters, so we have no way of knowing if Jackie has them," Auntie Rina says. "Seems like they're just random events to me. Purely coincidental."

"No, they're not. I'll bet you all a billion dollars that I'll hear from Jackie soon. You'll see. And when I hear from her, she'll tell me how much she loves my fashion designs."

"Don't hold your breath," my father says.

"What is it with you, Hank? You never say a word at the dinner table and now, when you do...," Mummy says.

"What did you mean by that remark?" I ask my father. "What did you mean when you said not to hold my breath? I'd like to know."

My father takes another frank from the platter and goes back to playing the silent game.

"I asked you a question."

My father still ignores me.

"What Daddy means is that Mrs. Kennedy is a famous person and might not have the time to answer letters from a little girl," Mummy says.

My father snickers, like he's enjoying his own private joke. I stand up to leave the table even though I haven't finished my dinner.

"I asked him, not you," I say as I push my chair in to the table. "I'd like to be excused. I'm going to call Anna Maria and share the good news with her. At least she'll be excited for me. And for the last time, I'm not a little girl!"

I want privacy, so I go down to the basement to dial up Anna Maria. We talk for a long while, and she wants to know every last detail, only there aren't that many to share. I hear my father coming down the stairs, so I quickly stretch the telephone cord into the cedar closet and shut the door. He turns on the television set and cranks up the volume.

"I think you should call up Susie Applegate and tell her that Jackie Kennedy is a customer in the store," Anna Maria says. "That'll get her goat."

"You think I should do that?"

"Absolutely. She's always trying to make you feel crummy. Now's your chance to get even with something big. Do it and tell her you're going to be designing all of Jacqueline Kennedy's clothes for the campaign and forever."

"But Anna Maria," I say. "Jackie hasn't answered any of my letters. If I say that, it'll be a lie."

"No it won't," Anna Maria says. "Not really. Are you still sending her designs?"

"Yes," I answer.

"And do you still plan on sending her designs if Senator Kennedy wins the nomination?"

"I guess," I say.

"Well, technically, then you're still designing for her. What little details Susie Applegate doesn't know won't hurt her."

"Okay, you convinced me. I'll do it. I'll call her."

"Call me back and tell me how it goes," Anna Maria says.

"Okay."

I dial Susie Applegate's telephone number and her mother calls her to the phone.

"Hi, Susie, it's Abby. I have the most exciting news, and I wanted to share it with…"

I do not finish my sentence. The door to the cedar closet springs wide open and my father grabs the telephone receiver from me and hangs it up. He yanks my ponytail like he wants to rip it clean from my scalp. His face is all black with anger, and his breath stinks from booze. He slaps me hard across the face and punches my shoulders.

"Yak, yak, yak, just like your mother. Don't you ever shut up, you miserable brat?"

"What did I ever do to you?" I gasp.

"You exist, that's what. You ruined my life," he says. "You and your rotten brother and your mother. I'm sick of this house and the store and of selling shoes. I'm sick of taking orders from those two upstairs. I'm sick of watching you and your brother turning out just like your mother's side."

I hurt. I whimper, but I will not cry. No matter what it takes, I will not cry. I will not give him that pleasure.

"Well, I'm glad for that. Who'd want to be like you? You're the worst father that ever lived. Me and Marty are on to you. We know how nice you are to strangers' kids and send Hanukkah cards with money to cousins we've never met. You never ask us what we like or what we do or how we feel. You don't know anything about your own kids."

"That's right," he says. "Because I don't care."

I walk around him and head for the stairs. I do not run.

"You'll never get any answers to your letters," he says.

I stop in my tracks mid-staircase.

"Your mother knows it, too."

"What do you mean?"

"Forget it," my father says as he turns on the television.

"Why don't you just leave, get out of here. Nobody will miss you. Ever. Even when you're dead and the worms eat you. Nobody will care."

I run to the Pink Palace and slam the door. I gather up as many dolls as I can fit in my arms and take them under the covers with me. I shut the light and bury my face in their soft bodies. Now I let my tears come, and I don't think they will ever stop. What makes things worse is that when I hold my dolls close, I am reminded that Mei is not among them.

19

Mazel Tov Means "Congratulations"

ABIGAIL LEAH SHAPIRO

January 21, 1960

Dear Jackie,

This is my first letter to you in the New Year and the new decade. 1960! Wow, it sounds so strange to say it out loud. Mummy says she's been having problems writing checks because she keeps writing 1959. Has the same thing happened to you?

By the way, mazel tov to you on Senator Kennedy finally making up his mind to run for president. It's okay that you didn't have the time to tell me first. I'll think of something else to tell the class during share time.

Jackie, I have a gift for you. I am sending you a sketch of a very special dress, only I didn't exactly design it for you in the first place. I designed it for my Uncle Max's girlfriend, Dolores

McAffee, who is going to become my new Aunt Dolores pretty soon.

Dolores sewed the dress out of red satin and used a red-and-green plaid material for the trim. She sent me a thank-you note with some photographs so I could see for myself how good everything came out. Dolores wears her hair in a bubble cut, and I think the toy company should make a Barbie doll with a hairdo like that. Maybe you should consider getting your hair cut like that, too. It would look very attractive on your head, I think. Anyway, Dolores knows that I want to be your personal fashion designer. I told her all about it. Dolores gave me permission to send her Christmas dress design to you. She said she'd be honored if you liked it and wanted to wear the same dress. Jackie, you could be twins with Dolores! But I don't think you'd have to worry about bumping into each other at parties. You probably have a different group of friends, especially because of what I told you about my Uncle Max and his shady past. So Dolores and I sincerely hope you will have this dress made for Christmas 1960, before everyone starts messing up their checkbooks again in January 1961.

Bye!
Your Friend in Fashion,
Abby

P.S. I finally got a Barbie doll. I got her the day of Christmas Eve, which was also the day of the first night of Hanukkah. She's okay. She's a lot different than my other dolls, especially the ones that come from foreign countries. She just doesn't wow me the way I thought she would.

P.P.S. I am now an official owner of a bra. Actually I have two bras. I told Mummy that I saw Anna Maria on Main Street and she bought them for me for Hanukkah. But that's not the truth. My soon-to-be Aunt Dolores bought them for me, but Mummy fell for my story-hook, line, and sinker. She was very annoyed at me at first for letting Anna Maria do that, and she said I'd have to rinse them out myself in the bathroom sink. But then she got over it. Now she washes them with the rest of the laundry. But she still won't admit that I really did need a bra.

P.P.P.S. Speaking of foreign dolls, I never found my Mei. I looked for her for days and weeks. My brother, Marty, even helped me for a while, but then he told me he had enough and he wouldn't help me anymore. Now there's snow on the ground. If she wasn't stolen by some mooching trick-or-treater, then I hope she's covered up with tons of leaves to keep her warm underneath the snow. I still worry about her every day.

P.P.P.P.S. Does your little girl, Caroline, have a Barbie doll? What do you think about a doll with big bosoms?

P.P.P.P.P.S. There's other stuff going on here in my house. Mummy's nerves might be the real reason why she's messing up the checkbook, and not because of the date change.

P.P.P.P.P.P.S. When I first met Dolores at my Uncle Max's nightclub, the Pink Elephant, I told her that she looked like a real live living Barbie doll. So I drew a picture of how she looked. I don't know if her outfit is your taste, but if you like it, it's yours, too.

20

Dribbles, Scribbles, and Shmibbles

"Who has news they'd like to share?" Miss Burns asks.

Susie Applegate's hand shoots way up and pulls her body out of her seat.

"Susie, the class appreciates that you always have so much to share, but perhaps somebody else could take the floor first today," Miss Burns says.

"What are you saying? That I can't share today? Because I have some very exciting news that will interest everyone," Susie says.

"No, Susie, that's not what I'm saying. Of course you can share, just let somebody else have the opportunity to go first for a change," Miss Burns says.

Susie pouts like she's sucked on one too many lemons. Miss Burns smiles sweetly at her. Teachers are a lot like actors. They have to pretend when they don't like a student. Especially the obnoxious, annoying ones, like Susie Applegate. I think Miss Burns deserves an Academy Award for Teachers.

"And the winner is . . . Miss Sally Burns, for the Most Patient Teacher of the Year!"

The only problem with that is that Miss Burns could not accept her award in one of her potato-sack dresses. Poor Miss Burns. No miracles happened in the clothing department for her over Christmas vacation. The fashion Santa did not come down her chimney.

Susie slinks back down in her seat.

"Stop staring at me, Abby," Susie says.

"Who, me? Staring? I'm not staring," I say. "And don't give me orders."

"I'll do whatever I like," Susie says with a snarl.

"Keep it up, Susie. You're cruisin' for a brusin'."

Susie's been on my case more than ever since January 2, 1960. That's when I called her to brag about Jackie Kennedy buying shoes in our store, the day when my father did what he did. When we returned to school after Christmas vacation, Susie got right up in my face and demanded to know why I phony phone-called her.

"I didn't," I tried to explain. "I called to tell you that I finally got my Barbie doll, that's all. But before I had the chance to actually say so, the phone went dead. We've been having a lot of trouble lately with the telephone wires in my neighborhood."

That was what I told her. It was only a half lie because on January 2, I did have my Barbie doll. That part was true. But I had to lie about the other half. What was I supposed to say? "Oh, Susie, I'm so sorry we got disconnected. But you see, my father was beating me up, so it really wasn't a good time to talk." After that I never bothered to tell her the news about Jackie. What for?

Three kids have already shared their news. Now someone is finishing telling a story about how they went to the emergency room with their little brother because he stuck a licorice jelly bean up his nose. Susie's waving her hand so high and fast that the temperature in the classroom has probably dropped a few degrees.

"Miss Burns, Miss Burns, my turn? May I go?" Susie asks.

It sounds like she's asking permission to go to the girls' room rather than share her wonderful news.

"Yes, Susie, you may take your turn."

Miss Burns picks up a paperweight from her desk and swooshes it back and forth and up and down. It's the Statue of Liberty inside a glass dome with liquid and snowflake-looking stuff. When she sets it back down on her desk, you can see a blizzard swirling around Lady Liberty in New York harbor.

Susie stands up and races to the head of the class. I really don't want to listen to her dribbles, so I take out my fashion-design sketchbook from my desk. I keep it with me all the time now. I turn to the pages of the two new designs I've been working on for Jackie. They're coming along quite nicely. I can see the improvement in my work. I really can.

"Something very exciting has happened to the Applegate family," Susie announces. "My father, who you all know is the manager of the First National Bank and Trust in Boston, just got a huge promotion. He's going to become president of the bank. That is the most important job of all in the whole bank. That means that Daddy will have a new office with a new desk and a new secretary. But he told Mother not to worry if his new secretary is pretty, because nobody is prettier than Mother."

I remind myself to tell Anna Maria about this. We can joke that maybe Mr. Applegate's new secretary will turn out to be Mrs. Riordan, my neighbor who Anna Maria called a flimsy.

Susie is wound up. Blah-blah-blah. I don't know how the girls in the Barbie doll club can stand her. She's so bossy. The membership has doubled since vacation. All of the girls who didn't have Barbies before Christmas got them as gifts. Susie asked Anna Maria to join, but she told her she wasn't interested. So then Susie said to Anna Maria, "Just as well. Even though your Barbie doll has lots of clothes, they aren't the real deal. They're just homemade imposters." Anna Maria said that she felt like tripping Susie in the playground. Anna Maria understands the meaning of loyalty.

I look up from my sketchbook. Susie is still blabbing away.

Now she's talking about getting a swimming pool and how her father said she could have an end-of-the-year sixth-grade party for the class if the pool is in the ground in time. More blah-blah-blahs.

"Miss Burns, Miss Burns," Susie says. "Abby is not being a good room twelve citizen. Her eyes and ears are not up here on me. Look at her, she's doing scribbles in her notebook. She scribbles all the time. Barbie clothes mostly, but they're not very good. Oh, oh, and sometimes she draws heads when she's supposed to be doing arithmetic. Just heads. And she names the heads. They're heads with names!"

Then Susie starts to laugh. And it's not her usual horsey laugh. This time she's braying like a donkey. Then everyone joins in and starts to laugh with her. I never would have thought that a donkey laugh could be so contagious. Scribbles, shmibbles, my foot! That's it! That's the final straw! Susie Applegate, now you're really going to get it!

"Miss Burns, if Susie's done, I have something I'd like to share with the class," I say.

"But Miss Burns, aren't you going to send Abby down to Principal O'Leary's office for rudeness?" Susie asks.

"I'll be the judge of who gets sent down to the office," Miss Burns says.

Miss Burns rubs her forehead like Mummy does when a killer migraine is coming on.

"Susie, take your seat. You've shared quite enough for one morning."

I guess Miss Burns isn't that good at acting after all. I sidestep Susie with my sketchbook under my arm and go to the head of the class. I take a deep breath.

"First of all, I do not scribble. I sketch. That's what fashion designers do. Yes, it is true that I design Barbie doll clothes, but that is just a small part of my business," I say.

"Business?" Miss Burns asks.

"Yes, I sell those designs. In fact, I have one customer who buys exclusively from me," I say. "And..."

Susie Applegate sticks her tongue out at me. Okay, that does it. Here it comes. I'm like a volcano with molten lava. I'm like a whistling teakettle with boiling water. I'm like an ice-cream soda that bubbles over because you blow hard into the straw.

"And I also design for women. Real women who are important. Real women who want to look like the talk of the town and feel good about themselves. Real women who wear one-of-a-kind clothes. In fact, I have a very famous client. Up until now it's been a secret. But today I'm in a sharing mood, so I will be generous and tell you."

"Yes, Abby, please do," Miss Burns says. "We'd love to hear."

"I'm proud to say that Jacqueline Lee Bouvier Kennedy is a client."

"Who?" Susie says. "Who's she?"

"Don't you know anything? We're talking about Senator Kennedy's wife. The Possible Future First Lady of the United States of America," I say directly to Susie.

"Abby, is this truly so?" Miss Burns asks.

"Oh yes, Miss Burns. You see, it all started when Jacqueline Kennedy purchased shoes from our family store. She heard that we had the reputation for selling the most fashionable shoes in all of Massachusetts. And confidentially, few people know this, but Mrs. Kennedy has unusually large feet. But my Uncle Morris had just the right shoes for her in stock. And so that's how we met and became close friends and discussed clothes and..."

This is so easy. I take a few facts that are true and I mix them with a few that aren't true. My story comes out as smooth as can be. My bowl of lies has no clumps at the bottom like the rubbery ones in Mummy's Jello-O. Suddenly I feel like I'm floating. Everyone in class is interested in my story. I'm important. I'm not just

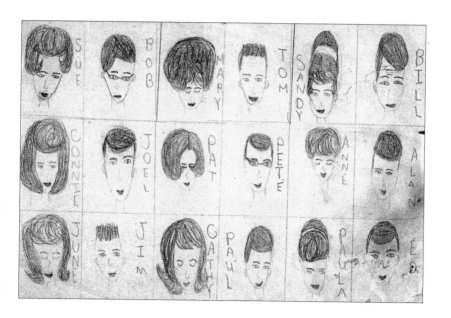

a nobody with a crazy family and a father who wishes I'd never been born. Right now I'm rising so high that I think nothing of Miss Burns asking permission to see my sketchbook. She takes it from under my arm. I watch her grin as she sees the page of heads with names. The grin turns to a smile as she looks at the newest designs for Jackie. I watch her smile broaden as she flips through the pages until she comes to the end of the sketchbook. And then the smile changes to a frown with knitted eyebrows and then to a wide-eyed face. Her eyes look so buggy big that I think they will pop right out of her head and roll onto the wooden classroom floor. Holy moly, stinky feet! How am I ever going to explain the sketches with the headings of "Everyday, Normal Miss Burns," "The Improved Miss Burns," and "Sexpot Miss Burns" to Miss Burns? This is not good. Not good at all. My goose is cooked. My goose is incinerated.

21
A New Client

"*Abby, please stay after dismissal,*" Miss Burns says at one minute to three.

I nod. I've been expecting this all day long. The bell rings and the class rushes out into the hallway. I sit in my seat until the last kid is gone. Then it's just me and Miss Burns all alone in the classroom. It feels like a showdown in a western movie. Miss Burns draws her gun first.

"That's a very accurate likeness of me you've drawn in your sketchbook." Miss Burns says these words very plain and matter of fact. Like she's teaching social studies.

"Please let me explain," I say.

"Abby, I'm not angry with you," Miss Burns says.

"You're not? Really?"

"Really. At first I was, but then I reminded myself that you are a very nice girl. You didn't draw those sketches of me to be mean or to poke fun," she says.

"No, I didn't. I swear," I say. "I like you a lot, Miss Burns, and I think you are a wonderful teacher, even though I hate arithmetic."

"Yes, I know," she says. "Heads with names."

"It's just that being a fashion designer, well, I can't help myself. I have a problem with impulse control. That's what my mother always says."

"My clothes are that bad?" she asks.

"Yup!"

Miss Burns sighs. Then she gets up from her desk and walks down my aisle. She sits on Susie Applegate's desk so we can talk woman to woman. "I hate my clothes, too," she says. "My mother selects them for me."

"So does mine," I say.

Everyday,
Normal
Miss Burns

The
Improved
Miss Burns

"But you're eleven and a sixth-grade student. I'm twenty-three years old and a professional teacher."

"Then you have to take a stand against your mother," I say. "I did when she said I couldn't possibly need a bra just because I'm still in grammar school."

"I can't believe I'm taking advice from a student, but you're right," Miss Burns says. "I need a completely new wardrobe."

I tear the pages from my sketchbook of "Everyday, Normal Miss Burns" and "The Improved Miss Burns."

Sexpot Miss
Burns

"Here, you take these," I say. "A gift from Abilea Coutures. Before and after sketches."

Miss Burns smiles.

"Actually, I know a good dressmaker," she says. "And by the way, I like the name of your business. It's very creative."

"It's from my name. Abigail Leah."

"Yes, I figured that out," Miss Burns says.

"Okay, then I guess I'll head on home now," I say.

"Not so fast," Miss Burns says. "I'd like the last page in the sketchbook as well."

I tear out my masterpiece of "Sexpot Miss Burns" and hand it over to my teacher.

"I really must get going," I say.

I grab my book bag and head to the open door to make my escape.

"Abby, wait!" Miss Burns says.

"Yes?"

Uh-oh! I hope she hasn't changed her mind and will now haul me down to Principal O'Leary's office.

"In the sketch of everyday me, why did you draw me with a turtleneck? I never wear turtlenecks," she says.

I take a deep breath and a gamble when I say what has to be said.

"I put you in a turtleneck because you should wear a turtleneck on account of your problem with...Mr. Polonski."

Miss Burns turns beet-red. Her ears are so red, they look like emergency exit signs in the movie theater.

"It's that obvious?"

"Yup," I say.

Miss Burns looks like she's going to start bawling.

"It's not so bad," I fib.

"Yes it is."

"Miss Burns, may I tell you about my Auntie Rina? My Auntie Rina is very wise. She always says that all you need in this life are kind thoughts, a genuine smile, and the perfect shade of red lipstick. All together, they'll make you look and feel like a million bucks! You already have kind thoughts and a genuine smile. You're just missing that third part. And when you get all new clothes, you'll be stunning. Just like a real fashion model."

Miss Burns nods and waves at me. I think she gets it.

"Thanks, Abby. See you tomorrow. Oh, and just one last thing," Miss Burns says.

"Don't worry," I say.

I pull an imaginary zipper across my lips and toss the imaginary key out the imaginary open window.

22

Roses Are Red, Apes Live in the Zoo, If Hank Split for Good, Why Is Mummy Still Blue?

I lay down my charcoal pencil when I hear Mummy come in through the back door. She's yelling and cursing. One of the words is on the absolutely forbidden list. Anna Maria blurted out that word the first time her mother served liver and onions for dinner. Her nonna Adelaide washed her mouth out with soap and then made her eat the liver and onions, anyway.

Mummy sits slumped at one of the kitchen chairs. She's still wearing her hat and coat. She props her elbows up on the table and supports her hanging head with her hands. I pick up an envelope that has dropped on the floor by her feet. It is addressed to my mother, Mrs. Betty Shapiro. The return address reads Miss Frances Shapiro, Post Office Box 5, International Falls, Minnesota.

I pull off Mummy's hat and help her with her coat. She's so pooped. She's looked knocked down, dragged out, run through the mill, ever since my father split without as much as a good-bye or a good riddance. It's been just about a month now. He got up, had breakfast, put on his hat and coat, and walked out the door.

"Who lives in Minnesota with our same last name?" I ask.

"Your aunt," Mummy answers.

"Aunt?"

"Your father's older sister."

"Oh."

I say that very calmly, like it's a fact I already know. But before this moment I had no idea that a Miss Frances Shapiro existed.

"She's quite a bit older than your father. She was already grown and on her own by the time he was born."

"And where exactly is International Falls, Minnesota?" I ask.

"Someplace that makes our New England winters seem warm," Mummy says.

"Have you ever met her?" I ask.

"No. Your father had a fight with Frances years before we were married and hadn't spoken to her since. But apparently that's all forgiven now that he's shown up at her doorstep."

I guess the mystery is officially solved. The Invisible Man has landed in International Falls, Minnesota. I wonder how he got there. Maybe it's taken him all this time to walk. Or maybe he thumbed a ride with a trucker. Or maybe he took a bus. I don't know and I don't care. He didn't even have the decency to write the letter himself to my mother.

"It's okay, Mummy. It's much better this way."

"He's never coming back," she says.

"Do you even care?" I ask.

"I'm so tired, Abby," she says. "Right now I don't know how or what I feel."

I give my mother a hug and a neck kiss and go down the hallway back to the Pink Palace. My new creation for Jackie is elegant with a capital E. I think it's ready to be mailed. It's a beautiful, short evening dress for a romantic dinner for two and a night on the town. I make a note next to the original drawing to consider this design for Miss Burns if anything works out with her and Mr. Polonski.

February 3, 1960

Dear Jackie,

Happy Valentine's Day even though it's eleven days away. I hope Senator Kennedy buys you roses. And I sincerely hope they will be the yellow ones. I know they cost a lot more money than the red ones, but I think they are worth every single penny.

Do you like candy? Last Valentine's Day I bought myself a candy-heart necklace with valentines written on them, like Be Mine and I Love You. I ate it all at once so Mummy wouldn't find out about it. That's because I ate one the year before, too, and when I went to the dentist, she yelled at me because I needed eight fillings. Last year I only had three cavities because I was brushing better.

How is the campaign going? Are you enjoying it? Do you have enough changes of outfits? You simply can't be left without a thing to put on your back. What would the reporters say? Well, today is your lucky day, Jackie. I have a Valentine's Day gift for you. It's quite special, so when you have your dressmaker whip it up it, please tell her not to change a thing. I mean it. I'm quite positive about how this dress should look. After all, I am the fashion designer.

The top is black stretchy lace and the

bottom should be a yellow taffeta. And not a pale yellow, but a really bright yellow, like the color of a canary. I gave you three strands of pearls, which I bet you already have because I can tell that Senator Kennedy is very thoughtful and buys you presents of jewelry all the time just because he loves you.

Bye!
Your Friend in Fashion,
Abby

P.S. By the way, how are your new shoes? Are they comfortable? They must be because Auntie Rina and Uncle Morris said they weren't returned to the store.

P.P.S. That purse you're carrying in the sketch is made of black beads and has a gold handle. The purse is big enough to hold a handkerchief and your favorite shade of lipstick. It's pink, isn't it?

P.P.P.S. Something really funny happened here, which was a good thing because Mummy has been very tense since my father abandoned us to move to International Falls, Minnesota. It snowed with freezing rain on top last Wednesday night. The next morning Marty went outside to clean the driveway with our new snow blower. Well, one minute Marty was pushing that thing and then the next he ran into the house screaming that there were parts of a dead body buried in the snow. You know what it was, Jackie? It was a tongue! But not a person's tongue. It was a cow tongue! Sam, the kosher butcher, delivered Mummy's order of meat before the storm and the tongue fell out of his truck. Auntie Rina said she was in the mood for a pickled tongue sandwich, so she called in the order. Yuck! Am I glad that thing never made it into the house, because it could have become part of Mummy's permanent menu. If that happened, I probably would have said that four-letter word that my best friend, Anna Maria, said when she had to eat liver and onions and when Mummy saw the letter that came today from my Aunt Frances that I never knew was alive.

P.P.P.P.S. I just looked up International Falls, Minnesota, in the World Book. It shares a border with a town in Canada called Fort Frances, which is so funny because Frances is the name of my aunt I just told you about. My father may have left because of something I said to him. It was a pretty awful thing to say. I wouldn't have said that awful thing if he hadn't gone berserk and beat me.

P.P.P.P.P.S. I don't know if you've gone to the beauty parlor yet to get a bubble cut. If you haven't, you can wear your hair in an updo like from the new sketch. Either way is okay. It really is none of my business to tell you what to do with your hair. But I do have opinions.

P.P.P.P.P.P.S. My brother, Marty, got really mad at all of us when we were howling over the frozen tongue. Mummy told him that we weren't laughing at him, but that the situation was funny. He didn't see it that way. He went up to his bedroom and slammed the door.

P.P.P.P.P.P.P.S. This is the longest letter I've ever written in my whole life. It took three hours. My hand is killing me. I'm a righty. What are you?

23
Hate Is a Four-Letter Word

"They did what?" I hear Mummy say to Effie.

My mother sounds upset. I can't hear Effie's response to my mother. She's a very soft-spoken person, unlike my mother with her high-pitched, screechy voice.

"Hi, what's going on?" I ask, pushing open the swinging door to the kitchen. I almost expect to be told that I should excuse myself during an adult conversation. But Mummy says, "Abby, sit down. You have to hear this. Effie has the most disgusting story to tell you."

"There's no blood and guts in this story, is there?" I ask. "Because if there is, save it for Marty and not for me."

"Just listen," Mummy says impatiently.

"I told your mama that I was going to do some shopping last week. You know, most of the stores downtown are running final sales. I went into Harrison's Ladies Apparel first."

I nod. We know the family that owns that store. They sell really nice sweaters and blouses. Their kids go to Hebrew school with me.

"What did you buy?" I ask Effie.

"She didn't buy anything," Mummy says.

"How come?" I ask Effie. "Didn't you see anything you liked?"

"She didn't buy anything, because they wouldn't let her buy anything," Mummy says.

I'm lost. "What do you mean they wouldn't let her buy anything? I don't get it."

"Effie didn't buy anything, because the mother, old lady Mrs. Harrison, wouldn't give her credit or let her put merchandise on layaway," Mummy says.

"Why not?" I ask.

"Because she's a Negro, that's why," Mummy screams.

Her face is all red, and the road-map vein in her head is throbbing. She is as mad as can be.

"I still don't get it."

"There are folks who don't like us," Effie says. "Because our skin is dark."

"That's plain stupid," I say. "That's like people not wanting to vote for Kennedy because he's Catholic."

"Effie, don't you dare hold back on me. What other stores did you go into to shop? You better tell me right this instant!" Mummy says.

"It's not that important. I shouldn't have told you. It's not your problem."

"Not my problem? Not my problem?"

Mummy is superupset now. She's repeating herself and walking around in circles in the kitchen. I am getting dizzy watching her spin around on black-and-white square floor tiles.

"How can you say that to me? How long have we been friends?"

"A long time."

"Who else? Who else wouldn't give you credit? Did you tell them all that we are one of your employers?"

"They all know I work for you."

"Just tell me who the 'they' are."

"All of them. All the ladies' clothing stores."

"Names, Effie," Mummy says. "I want names."

Mummy sounds like the FBI guy Eliot Ness from the television show *The Untouchables*.

"Archibald's, Lobdale's, Kaplan's, Boyajian's, DeGraff's, Kotlas's, and Mason's. That's it."

Auntie Rina always says that the names of the merchants' stores on Main Street sound like a list of immigrants coming over the ocean to Ellis Island.

"That's it, you say? That's all of them! That's every single ladies department store downtown. I am sickened—absolutely, positively sickened—by this," Mummy says.

She's stopped walking in circles, which is good because I went from dizzy to nauseous watching her.

"Get in the car," she orders Effie. "Abby, you, too."

Mummy guns the gas pedal and burns rubber peeling out of the driveway and onto Darlene Avenue. I've never seen her like this in my whole life. It's kind of exciting.

It's four thirty in the afternoon on Friday, the usual time when Mummy would drive Effie home. But I have a feeling we'll be making a few detours first. Mummy manages to drive us downtown without getting pulled over by a policeman. She was driving fifteen miles over the speed limit. She pulls into a space in front of Boyajian's, which is at the opposite end of Main Street from our store.

"This is our last stop. That's why I parked here," she says.

Mummy leads us, a parade of three, into the first store on the list. Harrison's Ladies Apparel. The owner of the store, old lady Mrs. Harrison, is behind the counter.

"Betty!" she says with a smile as she sees my mother come through the door. But the smile erases from her face when she realizes Effie is right behind my mother. Mummy gets right down to business.

"I understand you didn't treat this woman, Effie Johnson,

very well. Since when are you so wealthy that you turn away customers?" Mummy asks.

Mrs. Harrison looks uncomfortable.

"*Vos vilstu*?" she asks my mother in Yiddish.

"Oh no, speak in English. There'll be no secrets here," Mummy says.

"What do you want?" Mrs. Harrison asks in a very nasty tone.

"I want an apology for me and for Effie. How dare you dismiss her from your store! She is my personal friend and her credit is just as good as mine. I want you to apologize to us right now!"

Mrs. Harrison mumbles "I'm sorry." I can tell she doesn't really mean it but is doing it quickly because she doesn't want Mummy to make an even bigger scene. Some customers who were browsing hurry out of the store.

"Honestly, Betty, I don't know what's gotten into you. I'm happy to apologize if that's what you want, but you're overreacting. It was an honest mistake," Mrs. Harrison says.

"This is a *shande* and a *charpe*," Mummy says in Yiddish, a "shame" and a "disgrace." "Oh, and by the way, Ethel, your credit, your charge account has just been cancelled in our store. In fact, you're not welcome anymore as a customer. Go buy your shoes elsewhere."

Mummy grabs my hand and Effie's hand and leads us out of Harrison's Ladies Apparel. She moves to the right, and one by one we knock off every store on the list. Mummy is the hit woman of the downtown merchants. It's five thirty when we leave Boyajian's Casuals and get into the car.

"Thank you, Betty. That was very brave of you," Effie says.

Mummy bursts out crying. Effie leans over to hug her.

"I'm so sorry," Effie says. "With all you've been through in the last months, I shouldn't have let you do this."

Mummy wipes her cheeks with the backs of her hands.

"Are you kidding?" she says. "I feel fantastic! I haven't felt this good in years."

24
I, My Name Is Jackie

ABIGAIL LEAH SHAPIRO

March 2, 1960

Dear Mrs. Jacqueline Lee Bouvier Kennedy,

In case you have heard any nasty rumors going around about you, I might owe you an apology.

When I shared in class last month how you bought shoes from our family store, I did not leave out any details. Okay, so I might have said that you had large feet. But I didn't say it in a bad way. I just said it in a kind of matter-of-fact way because it was part of the story. The next thing I know, Susie Applegate is out in the playground making up a new jump rope rhyme about you. It went like this: "We like Jackie, she is sweet. Jackie double Dutches with her jumbo feet."

I stuck up for you. Really, I did. I told Susie Applegate that she was stupid and rude. But here's the problem. She said she told her cousin, who told all of her friends in her school, who told all of their cousins in other schools, and that everybody in Massachusetts would know that I told the whole world about your shoe size. Deep down inside, I don't really believe that will happen. But then again, my Auntie Rina always says that news travels fast in the Bay State. So I'm coming clean about it just in case.

Okay, then. I'm glad we cleared the air. May I go back to calling you Jackie? Thanks. I hoped you'd understand.

Bye!
Your Friend in Fashion,
Abigail Leah Shapiro

P.S. You can go back to calling me Abby.

P.P.S. I nearly forgot! I have some lovely new designs for you. I was so upset about you being mad at me that I got a farshtopte kop, which means in Yiddish "your head is all stuffed up like a toilet that needs a plunger when you used too much toilet paper." The first dress is fancy. It might even be too fancy for you. It's all beaded on the bodice and on the bottom for trim. I'm not sure why I had you walking a dog wearing this dress. Do you have a dog? I don't, but I wish I had one. But I'm not going to ask Mummy for a puppy right now, because Auntie Rina says she has too much on her plate. I'm wild about the second dress. That's kind of a joke because I was inspired to design it after watching a Tarzan movie. The off-the-shoulder part reminds me of Jane of the Jungle. See the the vine pattern on the dress? I don't know about you, Jackie, but some days I feel like swinging through the jungle on a vine with a bunch of chimps and yelling that Tarzan call, "Aaaah-ah-ah-ah-aaaah-ah-ah-ah-aaaah!"

P.P.P.S. On second thought, let's get rid of those puffy sleeves on the beaded dress. Tell your dressmaker it will look much better as a halter dress.

25
A Close Call

The piercing sound of a siren gets louder by the second. From the upstairs living room window I see an ambulance screech to a halt in front of Mrs. Whelan's house. A red light sweeps my face every few seconds. Neighbors are gathering outside on the sidewalk. Mrs. Whelan's Ford™ Fairlane™ is three houses down on the witches' lawn. The headlights are on, and they cast shadows on the big white Victorian.

"What's going on?" Uncle Morris asks over my shoulder.

"Not again," my mother says as she and Auntie Rina join us at the window.

"What a shame," Auntie Rina says. "Such a lovely woman and look what she's done...just wasted her life away with bad choices."

I feel Mummy bristle behind me.

"I've had plenty of heartbreak in my life," Mummy says, "but you don't see me drinking myself to death, do you?"

Mummy leaves the dining room table in a huff and goes downstairs. She's angry about everything. It's not just about my father anymore. It's like she's got a big, roaring bonfire inside her belly and another log gets tossed on the pile each time you annoy her or if she reads something in the newspaper about civil rights.

"We should see if we can help," says Auntie Rina.

"I'm going with you."

"No, Abby. You stay here. You're too young to see these kinds of things."

"I've seen her drunk before. I'm going with you. I like Mrs. Whelan."

"All right, then. Grab your coat. It's cold outside."

"I don't have to go, do I?" Marty asks.

"Nobody said you had to," I say.

"Good."

We go outside and join up with Mr. Lane and his mother across the street.

"What happened?" Auntie Rina asks.

"Poor Gladys. She's been at it quite heavily all week. Tuesday was her wedding anniversary. Would have been their twenty-fifth had Joe lived," Mr. Lane says very sympathetically. "She's been in the house for days drinking herself into a stupor. Mother and I brought over soup, but she shushed us away at the back door. She said she just wanted to be left alone."

"And the car?" Auntie Rina asks, gesturing toward the witches' lawn.

"She managed to drive herself to the package store for some refills, but on the way home, well, as you can see for yourself, she miscalculated her driveway," Mr. Lane says.

"Who called for the ambulance?" I ask.

"Bronislawa and Ludmila," Mrs. Lane says.

The ambulance driver instructs everyone to clear the driveway. We step off to one side.

"Who are Bronislawa and Ludmila?" I ask Auntie Rina.

"The *tsvey shvester*," the 'two sisters,' she whispers to me. "*Feh!*"

I turn to ask Mrs. Lane a question.

"Do they speak English?"

"Of course. But their accents are thick. It takes some getting used to," she says.

"Bronislawa and Ludmila are angels," Mr. Lane says. "If it weren't for those two women, who knows? They followed Gladys back to her house. But Gladys lost her keys between their house and hers. So she smashed the glass pane of the door to let herself inside. Only she did it with her fists and her forehead. Bronislawa and Ludmila wrapped up her wounds. Then they called for an ambulance."

The medics carry Mrs. Whelan out on a stretcher. There are bandages around both of her wrists and around her head. I can see red areas where blood is seeping through. I feel faint and lean against Auntie Rina.

"Breathe in deeply," Auntie Rina tells me.

The siren is turned back on and the ambulance speeds away. One by one the neighbors go home. The show is over.

Auntie Rina takes my hand and we cross the street.

"I never should have let you come with me," Auntie Rina says. "You didn't need to witness something like that at your age."

"I'm growing up. Just because I'm the baby of the family doesn't mean that everybody has to treat me like one."

"I know that, Abby."

"Auntie Rina?"

"Yes?"

"Maybe you're wrong about those two sisters, Bronislawa and Ludmila. Maybe they aren't witches. Maybe they're not so bad after all. Look what they did tonight. They did a *mitzvah*, a 'good deed.'"

Auntie Rina has never raised her voice to me in my entire life—until now.

"You might be growing up, but you don't know everything," she says. "Those two sisters? Angels they're not," Auntie Rina says, goes into the house, and leaves me standing on the porch.

26
Stir Up the Pot of Bad Memories

I slip into bed next to Auntie Rina. I don't know what time it is. It's still dark outside. The only noises in the house are the furnace rumbling and Uncle Morris from the bedroom next door sawing wood with his snoring.

"You up?" I whisper.

"Have been for hours," Auntie Rina says.

"Me too. I didn't sleep a wink. I couldn't stop thinking about Mrs. Whelan."

Auntie Rina yawns and stretches. She reminds me of a bear that isn't ready yet to come out of the cave at the end of winter.

"I know. Poor Gladys. I feel like I've let her down. I should have noticed that her drapes were closed all week. I should have realized that she was in trouble. Then maybe I could have prevented this all from happening."

"Don't blame yourself," I tell Auntie Rina. "It isn't your fault. You couldn't have known. You're not friends with her the way me and Anna Maria are. She's just a nice neighbor. Face it, you're strangers."

Auntie Rina sighs.

"I know, Abby. You're right, but I just can't help but feel guilty."

"I love you, Auntie Rina," I say.

"I love you, too. And I'm so sorry I yelled at you yesterday."

"It's okay."

"No, it's not okay," Auntie Rina says.

We lie snuggled together for a few minutes, neither of us saying a word.

"Where's your sketchbook?" Auntie Rina finally says. "It's Sunday. Don't you want to discuss fashion today?"

"No, I don't. I want to talk about other things," I say.

"Like what?"

"I want to talk about us. I want to talk about the family. I have so many things I need to know. I need to understand stuff," I say.

"You were right yesterday when you said we shouldn't treat you like a baby. But that's hard not to do. Life can be so difficult. I guess trying to keep you a child as long as possible is just another way of protecting you from life's hurts."

"Nobody in this family ever talks about anything. My father walked out, and you and Uncle Morris are acting like nothing happened. You haven't mentioned his name once in a conversation. I don't think that's normal."

"Do you miss your father?" Auntie Rina asks.

"No, I do not. But that's not the point. Just answer my questions."

"Fine. What do you want to know?"

"Let's start with the big one. Why do we all live together in this house?" I ask.

"It's complicated."

"Try me."

Auntie Rina sits up in bed and leans over me to turn on the night-table lamp and to get her eyeglasses.

"I suppose the best way to start is to go all the way back to when we were kids. By that I mean me, Uncle Max, Uncle Morris, and your mother. You do know that Bubbie Lena was a widow when she was pregnant with your mother?"

"Yes, I knew that," I say.

"Imagine what life was like for her trying to manage three young children in a new country with one more on the way. She had to feed us, provide a home, so she ran a little dry goods store for immigrant women to buy a little of this and a little of that," Auntie Rina says. "We were very poor. We were poor in the Old Country, but it was worse here. Your grandmother was all alone. She had difficulty coping."

"What do you mean? That she was sad all the time?" I ask.

"That's exactly what I mean. She was depressed. But in those days things like that were kept secret. So much of the family responsibility fell upon my shoulders. I was a kid myself. But when I wasn't in school, I had to be the mother. I had to cook and clean and take care of a baby sister and keep my brothers out of trouble. Believe you me, that was no easy task."

"I can understand Uncle Max getting into trouble, but Uncle Morris, too?"

"He was just as bad. He worshipped your Uncle Max, so he followed him around and did whatever he did. When they were in grade school, they were picked up by the police more times than I care to remember. Stealing, rolling dice, playing hooky from school. The truant officer was always at our door. You name it, those boys did it, along with their cohorts."

"What does that mean?" I ask.

"That means the neighborhood boys were just as bad. Sy and his brothers were part of their gang of hoodlums."

This is the perfect opportunity for me to slightly change the subject and bring it around to Sy, but Auntie Rina keeps on talking.

"I had to drop out of school after sixth grade," she says. "To this day that is my biggest shame, that I never got a high school diploma. Everything I know in this world, I learned from the school of hard knocks. That means I had no formal education. Living a hard life was my teacher."

I kiss Auntie Rina's soft cheek.

"I didn't know you had to drop out of school. I'm sorry about that."

Auntie Rina smiles at me. She has a pink hairnet on over hair curlers. She sets her hair in between beauty parlor appointments. Auntie Rina always says that she is a plain gal, but to me she's beautiful.

"Anyway, the point is that I tried to keep the family close. And for the most part we were. As the years passed, all we knew was work and caring for our mother."

"Tell me how Mummy met my father."

"It was right at the start of the war. They met at a dance, and shortly after he was called up by the navy. They wrote letters to each other over the years that he was in the South Pacific. Your mother was getting older, so I encouraged her to get married when your father returned home. I didn't want her to miss out on chances the way I had. If you don't pay attention, life can pass over you, just like that wagon wheel passed over my foot. I thought they'd be happy, but it didn't work out. You see, they were strangers. They only knew each other through letters. They'd spent very little real time together, and when they did, well, it wasn't so good. Plus, there were other issues," Auntie Rina says.

"You mean my father's drinking?" I ask.

"Yes, but as I said, there were other issues as well."

"Like what?"

"Me, your uncles, we were all your mother knew. She was very dependent upon us. We only had her best interests at heart, so we took care of everything for her. That was a big mistake on our part. Uncle Morris thought that building this house would be the perfect solution, but it wasn't. Her loyalty to us, her family, was greater than her bond to her husband. That's not a good way to start a marriage. And if I'm going to be completely truthful here, I admit that Uncle Morris, and myself included, weren't always so warm to your father. He was a difficult man to like. So we kept him at arm's length, and what happened was that he felt like an outsider. An outsider who was dependent upon us for work, for food, a home. For everything. I can understand how he felt trapped."

"I don't think you feel guilty about Mrs. Whelan. I think you feel guilty about Mummy," I say.

"I made a mess of your mother's life," Auntie Rina says. "I only hope in time she can forgive me."

"Auntie Rina?" I ask.

"Yes, doll?"

"How come you never married Sy? Was he your boyfriend?"

"Sy? Where did that come from? How did he get into this conversation?" Auntie Rina asks.

"I know he's been in love with you forever. I know he's still in love with you," I say.

"Who told you that?"

"Sy did."

"He what!"

Auntie Rina is upset. Her voice is raised to the point of yelling. Uncle Morris stops snoring in his bedroom next door.

"Shhh," I whisper. "I think we woke up Uncle Morris."

"Never mind that," Auntie Rina snaps. "You tell me right now what Sy said to you."

"He didn't exactly say it to me. I heard him say it to you in so many words the last time he came by the house with Uncle Max, back in November. I've been wanting to ask you about it since then, but I figured you'd get mad."

Auntie Rina tosses off the covers and climbs over me to get out of bed.

159

27
Mazel Tov Times Two

ABIGAIL LEAH SHAPIRO

April 9, 1960

Dear Jackie,

Congratulations again! My Auntie Rina told me that you are going to have a baby. Wow, that's big news. Almost as big as Senator Kennedy running for president. My mother won't be having any more babies. First of all, she's too old. And second of all, even if she could, she has no husband. She's going this afternoon to see a lawyer and find out what she has to do to get the divorce ball rolling. The problem will be in communicating with my father, who, as I told you in an earlier letter, split for good for International Falls, Minnesota, to live with his sister, who I didn't even know was alive as a person. He won't answer any of Mummy's letters or come to the phone when she calls. He's trying to pretend that none of us ever existed. Mummy just wants to speak to him. She doesn't understand why he won't talk to her, because she made it very clear in her letters that she doesn't want anything from him, like alimony. Uncle Max and Uncle Morris have money and will take care of us.

But as far as everything else goes, life on Darlene Avenue is okay. Mummy is spending a lot of time at Democratic headquarters downtown. She is probably Senator Kennedy's number one fan, except, of course, for you, Jackie. She volunteers her extra time to work for his campaign. She wears a button on her coat that says Kennedy for President, Leadership for the 60s. She also stuck some signs on our front lawn. Actually, she put in about five, and Uncle Morris told her it wasn't necessary to go overboard like that. He said two signs with different slogans would be enough. So Mummy stuck the extras in a neighbor's lawn. She felt like a naughty kid doing it because they support Vice President Richard Nixon. Sometimes she stays late at headquarters to make telephone calls to voters or to help distribute leaflets. Mummy bought a whole bunch of new clothes to wear and even went to the dentist to have a tooth fixed. She's beginning to look like her old self again. Auntie Rina said that working for Senator Kennedy's campaign has been like a shot in the arm for her.

Mummy says that Senator Kennedy should be president because he will fight to end poverty and make sure that Negroes have equal rights. She's been very proud of herself since that day she stood up for our housekeeper, Effie, who wasn't treated too nicely by some people that Mummy knows. I'm proud of her, too, because she did something she believed in and didn't back down. She never did brave stuff like that when my father lived here. She said that being sad all the time zapped all her energy. Mummy said that Senator Kennedy might even come to town and that if he does, she'll take me to the rally. I hope that you will be there, too. We could discuss our favorite topic...fashion!

Okay, enough chitchat. The House of Abilea Coutures is proud to present two maternity dresses special for Mrs. Jacqueline Kennedy. I didn't know exactly how to draw a pregnant lady, so I just made the dresses fuller in the tummy. As you know, I have always sketched you with a very small waist. I bet you hope you have a boy. Then you'd have one kid for each hand and one of each kind, just like me and my brother, Marty.

Bye!
Your Friend in Fashion,
Abby

163

P.S. My brother, Marty, is doing a little better. Mummy put her foot down. Marty can't hang out with his friends Todd and Harry anymore because they got into trouble lighting hydrogen soap bubbles in the woods. Some glass exploded and Marty got cut up. After she screamed at him for nearly losing an eye, Mummy hugged him and said she forgave him if he promised never to do anything idiotic like that again. Marty hugged her back and said he was sorry. I think that's a good sign, don't you? Mummy says that Marty's friends Todd and Harry were a bad influence on him. She says it's really not Marty's fault, because a teenage boy needs a real father. Uncles might be second best, but they're not the same thing.

P.P.S. Since my last letter my Uncle Max's girlfriend, Dolores McAffee, has become Mrs. Max Cohen. They got married on Saint Patrick's Day because Dolores is Irish. Auntie Rina thinks that she's after his money because she looks young enough to be Max's daughter. She's worried about what other people are going to say. But I told her to give Dolores a chance because she is so nice and really loves Uncle Max. I think Auntie Rina might be a little jealous that I've got a new aunt who is so pretty. But here's the best part—Dolores is going to have a baby, just like you! If Auntie

Rina has something to say about it, she's kept it to herself. I'm super excited. Even Mummy and Marty smiled when they heard the news. I've never held a baby before. Their baby will be my first first cousin. Aunt Dolores says that when I get a little older, I can babysit.

28

Why Is This Night Different From All Others?

Upstairs and downstairs have been cleaned and scrubbed from top to bottom. All of the dishes, pots and pans, silverware, and glasses have been changed. Everything has to be perfect for Passover. Last night we did the search for the *chametz* all over the house. For the ceremony Mummy took ten little crusts of bread and placed them in different rooms of the house. Then we lit a candle to search for them and used a feather to sweep them up onto a newspaper. When all of the crusts of bread were collected, Mummy took them outside to burn. Since I'm learning Hebrew, I read and recited the prayer.

Tonight is the first Seder and Mummy is at the store until closing. I'm helping Auntie Rina in the upstairs kitchen. She's making the *matzoh* balls for the soup. She is a much better cook than Mummy. My job is to polish the silver holiday candlesticks.

"What you're doing is very important," Auntie Rina says.

I've polished these candlesticks many times. They're very beautiful and came from the Old Country. "I know. Are you going to give me another lecture about rules and customs and *Bubbie* Lena?"

"No, I'm not going to lecture you. But I will tell you a story.

It's really the rest of the story about our coming to this country," Auntie Rina says. "Or better yet, it's the beginning of the story."

"First give me a clean cloth, please," I say. "This one is all black already from rubbing."

Auntie Rina gets me a *shmatte*, a "clean rag," and turns the heat up on the burner where the *matzoh* balls cook in the big pot of chicken soup. Then she sits with me at the kitchen table.

"Remember I told you about a pogrom, a massacre in Vilna."

"Yes. You had to hide in a pickle barrel," I say.

"These candlesticks were hidden in that barrel with me. They are pure silver and worth a lot to some for their monetary value. But they are worth much more to us for their religious significance, for the carrying on of tradition. They belonged to your great-grandmother, and one day they'll belong to you."

"I never knew that you had to hide them. Why didn't you tell me that part of the story?" I ask.

"Because there's more to the story, and it wasn't something that should reach a child's ears. But you're not such a little girl anymore," Auntie Rina says. "My father was the one who hid the candlesticks with me in that barrel. I will never forget how he lifted the lid and told me not to make a sound. He said that everything would be all right. I heard him say the same thing to your uncles, who were hiding in cupboards. And then there was a lot of noise and screaming and commotion as the intruders broke into the house. I could hear my mother pleading and my father trying to reason with them. Then there was wailing, moaning, crying like you can't imagine. It was coming from my mother. I raised the barrel cover and saw her on the floor holding on to her belly while she rocked back and forth. Lying next to her was my father. Dead. They killed him trying to protect his home and his pregnant wife. They killed him because he said there was nothing of value in the house. When the ordeal was over, many Jews in

Vilna were dead. Many women became widows. It was not such a new story over the years in a place where you were not welcome. Anyway, the rabbi was called and my father was buried the next morning. That same night we left my father behind in the cemetery and boarded a steamship to come to America."

Auntie Rina removes her eyeglasses to rub her eyes. She looks so tired, like telling the story drained all of her strength.

"I always thought your father was a carpenter who died in an accident. I thought it happened here."

"He was a carpenter, and I suppose saying it was an accident is better than telling a child that he was murdered," Auntie Rina says. "I'm telling you this story so you'll understand that a person's family is their fortress and that you must live by your traditions or else you will forget who you are. This is why my skin crawls whenever I see those two women, the two sisters. And maybe you're right. Maybe they did a *mitzvah*, "a good deed," when they helped Gladys Whelan. And maybe they personally never did anything against Jewish people, but their kind did. Their kind killed my father. And I just can't help the way I feel. Leopards don't change their spots."

"Auntie Rina, I have to tell you something," I say.

I want to tell her what's lying heavy on my heart.

"Not now, Abby," she says as she jumps up to turn off the stove.

While we were talking, the chicken soup boiled over onto the stove and dripped down to the floor.

"Step back," Auntie Rina says. "I don't want you to get scalded."

She wets a few dishrags and kneels down on the floor to mop it up.

"*Tsk, tsk*, what a mess I made!" she says.

No, Auntie Rina, I think I'm the one who made the mess.

And even if you can't stand those women, I still know what I did was wrong. It's been eating away at me for six months and I don't know what to do about it. A Jewish holiday might be starting tonight, but right now I wish I was Catholic, like Anna Maria. Then I could just go to church and tell Father Joe what I did, and he'd tell me to say some Hail Marys and I'd be forgiven. I wish it was that easy.

29
Headless Barbie

"My nonni says you are just like the shoemaker's daughter," Anna Maria says.

We are playing Barbies in the Pink Palace and eating a snack of cream cheese and blueberry jam on *matzoh* and Jordan almonds for dessert.

The Jordan almonds are from Anna Maria's cousin Rosemary's wedding to Rocco. She said it's an Italian custom to give them as wedding favors. There are five different-colored candy-coated almonds piled up in a small pillbox-shaped box that doesn't have a lid. There's even a silky ribbon tied around the box. Anna Maria said you're supposed to put the candy under your pillow at night and make a wish before you go to sleep. Then in the morning your wish will come true, or hopefully will come true that day or someday soon.

Anna Maria likes to suck off the candy shell and then eat the whole plain almond. I like to chew mine up quickly. I like the sound of the crunch and the taste of the sugar chewed with the nut. The Jordan almonds are technically not kosher for Passover, even though they are not made from bread, which is forbidden during the holiday. But since it's the last day of Passover, I bend the rules a little.

"What does that mean, shoemaker's daughter?" I ask Anna Maria.

"It means that you design all these wonderful Barbie doll clothes for me, but your Barbie is practically naked."

My best friend is right. My Barbie has no clothes except for the black-and-white strapless bathing suit she came with in the Dressed for Swim and Fun box. And the thing of it is, I don't care. The fun for me is in designing the clothes. And I love that Nonna Adelaide sews them up so pretty. I'm always happy when I see that Anna Maria's Barbie is wearing a new outfit. I am never jealous. Nonna Adelaide has offered many times to sew up another set of outfits for me, but I told her thanks, but no thanks. I really don't want them. I can always borrow Anna Maria's doll clothes if I want to. But I never want to. I'm just not that interested.

I've thought about this a lot, and this is how I feel. My Barbie doll turned me into a liar. It all began when I told that first little lie to Mummy about writing to Jackie Kennedy as a school pen pal project. I had to lie because she'd never mail my letters if she knew I wanted to charge money to a famous person. And why did I want to charge Jackie Kennedy? Because Mummy said that I needed to earn the money for a Barbie. And of course, there's the whole thing about Barbie's bosoms and about Mummy saying I didn't have any bosoms, so then I had to lie about getting the bras. By the time I picked up my Barbie on Christmas eve and saw her for the first time, I didn't feel a thing. Nothing. That never happens to me when I get a new doll. I always love them from the get go.

"You want more *matzoh* and cream cheese and jam?" I ask Anna Maria.

"No. I'm stuffed," she says. "That *matzoh* fills you up fast."

Auntie Rina always says that *matzoh* is so heavy, it's like eating a lead balloon and sinking to the bottom of the ocean.

"I'm bored," I say to Anna Maria.

"What do you want to play instead?"

"What I mean is I'm bored with Barbie. I'm sick of her hair

and her stupid, curly bangs. I'm sick of her eyes and the way they are stuck looking off to the right. Why did they make her look like that? Nobody in real life walks around looking like that all day long."

Anna Maria laughs.

"Now that you mention it, you're right! It is kind of odd. What does Barbie do if she needs to see something off to the left? Turn counterclockwise?"

Anna Maria loves her doll. I'm glad she didn't take offense at my Barbie insult.

"I'm sick of her tiptoes, too," I say. "Barbie is supposed to be a teenager, but the only shoes she can wear are spikes. What teenager do you know who wears high heels all day long? What if she wants to wear sandals or sneakers? She can't. That is the stupidest thing I've ever seen."

"They could make blue canvas high heels with rubber soles," Anna Maria says. "Could you picture playing badminton wearing them?"

"I think I'll give my Barbie to you," I tell Anna Maria. "I don't want her anymore."

"Thanks, but you don't really want to do that."

"Yes I do. I mean it. I really do. I'm not just saying that."

I watch Anna Maria twirl her bangs. She's thinking. She's coming up with some brilliant idea. The last time she did this, it ended up with me forming Abilea Coutures. Her bangs are in corkscrews. Her brain is working overtime.

"I've got it. This might be my best idea ever!" she says. "Let's give your Barbie a makeover."

"Uh-uh. I'm done with makeovers. Look what happened with Miss Burns. I could have gotten detention for the whole school year."

"But you didn't, and now she's dressing cute with new clothes and makeup, and she and Mr. Polonski are exchanging more words than just good morning in the hall, if you've noticed," Anna Maria says.

"Yuh, I've noticed."

I actually feel pretty good about that. I'm like the cupid of sixth grade. Somebody in Anna Maria's class said they saw Miss Burns and Mr. Polonski out at the movies last Saturday night. Or it could have been them. The girl couldn't be one hundred percent positive because it was dark in the theater, but she's pretty sure it was Miss Burns and Mr. Polonski sharing a large tub of popcorn.

"Let's change your Barbie into somebody else. Let's change her into some other doll that nobody else has."

"Have anyone in mind?" I ask.

"Oh yeah! Just a certain someone who you've been designing the most fabulous clothes in the world for. Just a certain someone who'd be *the* doll that nobody else has. Just a certain someone who's going to be the next First Lady of the United States!"

"We don't know that for sure," I tell Anna Maria. "Senator Kennedy hasn't been nominated yet."

"But he will be. Everybody likes him. Come on, Abby. Let's do it. You know you want to. My nonni will sew some outfits from your Abilea Coutures line. Susie Applegate will turn green with envy when she sees what you've done."

I think this through for about five whole seconds.

"Okay. Let's make a list of what we have to do. It's so important to be organized."

"Oh, I agree," Anna Maria says, reaching for pen and paper from my desk. "What's first? You talk and I'll write."

"The first thing is to dye her hair. She needs to be a brunette. Number two is to give her a haircut. We could just cut the ponytail to shoulder length, or..."

"Or what? What?" Anna Maria asks.

"Or we could cut it into that really cute hairstyle that my Aunt Dolores has, the bubble. I already wrote to Jackie suggesting she cut her hair like that," I say. "So let's do it for her."

"I love it!" Anna Maria says.

"And number three, change the makeup."

"How are we going to do that?"

"You'll see when we get to it. It'll be easy," I say.

I take out my worst pair of white socks from the bureau and tell Anna Maria to wrap one around Barbie's neck to use like a beauty-salon cape. While she does that, I go to the kitchen and get the shoeshine kit from the cabinet under the sink.

"I know exactly what to do," I say as I shake the liquid bottle of brown shoe polish. "I've watched Mummy getting a rinse at the beauty parlor a million times. You start from the roots and work your way down. Your job is to hold Barbie still."

Anna Maria grabs Barbie by the waist and legs as I turn the bottle of shoe polish upside down. I carefully roll the ball all over the crown of Barbie's head. Then I start on the ponytail. I am very careful to tip the shoe polish back and forth. This way the liquid flows but doesn't drip. Slowly but surely Barbie turns from a blonde into a brunette.

"Wow, that looks good," Anna Maria says.

"We have to let the shoe polish dry before we cut her hair."

"Get your hair dryer. It'll take forever to dry on its own. Feel how thick her hair is."

We stick Barbie under the bonnet of my portable hair dryer. Anna Maria is right. The hair dries quickly this way.

"Scissors," I say as I stick my hand out with a flat palm.

"You sound like a surgeon talking to a nurse," Anna Maria says, rummaging through my desk. "All you've got are these paper scissors. They won't work. Got any sewing scissors?"

"Yuh. Maybe."

I bound up the front staircase two steps at a time and take a pair of scissors from Auntie Rina's mending kit. I run my finger over the edge. Sharp, very sharp. I slowly walk back downstairs.

"Ready, Doctor?" Anna Maria asks.

"Yes, Nurse Tucci. Hold Barbie's legs with your right hand and pull her ponytail straight up with your left."

"Yes, Doctor Shapiro. I'm ready. The patient is ready."

I zero in on the base of the ponytail and cut through the thick vinyl hair with three big snips. Doll-hair clippings rain all over the hot-pink shag rug.

"So far so good," Anna Maria says.

"Shake her out to get rid of any loose hairs."

Anna Maria twirls Barbie around like a ballerina and flips her over like a high-wire acrobat. A huge clump of hair from the top of her head plops on my thigh.

"Holy cow!" Anna Maria says. "It came out from the roots! Barbie's got a monk fringe haircut!"

Barbie has bangs, side hair in the front, and back fringe. That's it. Anna Maria is right. This hairstyle is not a bubble and doesn't come close to anything I've ever seen in a fashion magazine. No woman in 1960 wants to be totally bald on the top of her head and look like a religious man.

"Abby, say something!"

"I can't. I'm in shock!"

"Okay, don't panic. Let's fix her. Get some glue," Anna Maria says.

"I'm out of glue."

"Think of something else that's sticky. But don't say honey."

"I can't think of anything," I say. "Masking tape?"

"Forget it. Does Marty have any glue in his bedroom?"

"Nah, he gave up building models. Oh, but wait, wait a minute! He's got something else. He's got something that just might work. Stay right here."

"I'll be right here taking care of the patient."

I run upstairs and into Marty's bedroom, where I am not allowed to be if he's not home. But these are special circumstances. I swipe the tube of gunk that holds up Marty's boy bangs all day long.

"I've got Marty's whiffle stick," I say, running back into the Pink Palace. "I think it'll do the trick."

"Cover the whole bald spot."

I smear the top of Barbie's bald spot like I'm spreading hot melted butter on a stack of buttermilks at the International House of Pancakes. There's not a speck of scalp unslathered.

"Do it," Anna Maria orders. "Patch it up!"

Anna Maria hands me the clump of hair she's neatly piled and squared off at the bottom. I press it down firmly and it stays, for about thirty seconds. Then it avalanches down Barbie's skull onto her shoulders. If she were wearing a coat, it would look like a fur collar.

"Try again," Anna Maria says. "Maybe you didn't use enough whiffle stick. Put gobs on this time."

I wear the whiffle stick practically down to a nub. It's turned from white to brown from rubbing so hard into the shoe polish–stained scalp. This time it works no better. The hair slides down with the sticky gobs attached. Doll hair must be a lot heavier than human hair.

"Forget it, it's no use. I screwed her up big time. Do me a favor. Next time I decide to mutilate a Barbie doll with a haircut, remind me to undo the ponytail first. That was a dumb, dumb idea to clip it off at the rubber band."

"Never say die," Anna Maria says. "When all else fails, use a stapler."

Before I can protest, Anna Maria picks up the hair, slaps it back on Barbie's bald spot, grabs a stapler from my desk, and pumps half a dozen staples into Barbie's neck and scalp.

"There, that ought to do it," she says. "That hair's going no place now."

Anna Maria puts the stapler back on my desk and swishes her hands back and forth. I know she's pleased with herself, but she looks like she's conducting an orchestra.

"That's just great," I say. "We really made a one-of-a-kind doll, we sure did! She's a cross between the Bride of Frankenstein and Moe from the Three Stooges."

"Don't be ridiculous," Anna Maria says. "Moe doesn't have bosoms."

"Minor detail," I say, "but they've got the same ugly haircut."

Anna Maria shakes her head sadly in agreement.

"Give me a ribbon from a Jordan almond box," I say. "Jackie wears a lot of scarves."

I place it over the wad of stapled hair and tie it under the doll's chin.

"It looks like a chin strap to a drum majorette's hat," Anna Maria says.

Anna Maria takes baton-twirling lessons on Saturday mornings.

"It's my fault for suggesting the makeover. I'm sorry I got so bossy. In the future don't ever listen to a thing I say."

"Never mind. You weren't the one who did the cutting. I guess there's no beauty school in my future."

"Now what?" Anna Maria asks while chewing a bare Jordan almond.

As I watch her dump the small candy box into the garbage I get a brilliant idea.

"How many of those candy pillboxes do we have in the trash can?" I ask.

Anna Maria takes them out to count.

"Ten, not including the two boxes of Jordan almonds we haven't touched yet," she says.

I stick one of the pillboxes on top of Barbie-Jackie's head. It's a perfect fit on account of the extra padding from the stapled hair. I take out my box of magic markers from my desk.

"Nurse Tucci, start coloring," I say. "We've got the cure."

By the time we're done coloring, Barbie-Jackie has a new wardrobe of ten colorful pillbox-shaped hats.

"I think this will catch on as a new fashion statement," I say to Anna Maria. "And besides, it solves the problem."

"*Oui, oui,*" she says. "Now what about the makeup?"

"Wait here."

"Why do you keep saying that? Where am I going?"

I return from the bathroom with an emery board.

"Watch this," I say to Anna Maria as I sand off Barbie's original, bright-red lipstick. "Jackie's color is more of a rosy pink."

"Crayon?"

"No. Ballpoint pen. It needs to be permanent."

I shake the pen with the pink cap a few times to get the ink moving smoothly. I press against the outline of the lower lip. Nothing. I shake the pen again and tap it hard against the leg of my desk.

"That ought to do it," I say. "Tip Barbie-Jackie's head back, like she's in the dentist's chair."

I press firmly once more along the outline of the lower lip. Suddenly the tip of the ballpoint pen snaps off and ink gushes forth like from a freshly drilled oil well. It spurts up into Barbie-Jackie's perfect little nostrils, all over her cheeks, and runs into her ears.

"Turn her the other way!" Anna Maria shouts.

Stupidly, I listen, and ink runs all over Barbie-Jackie's chin, neck, and all the way down to her imaginary *pupik*, her "belly button." I blot the mess with the sock we used as a beauty parlor cape.

"That ink doesn't look pink to me," Anna Maria says. "I think you had the wrong cap on the pen."

Barbie-Jackie is orange. Bright orange. Clown-in-the-circus, curly-haired-wig orange.

"We could color in the rest of her body so it would all be the same," Anna Maria says. "But I've never seen a bright-orange-skinned person. Have you?"

"Nope."

"Now what?" Anna Maria asks.

"Now nothing. I'm done. I don't care. Like I told you, I was sick of her, anyway."

"You have a very positive attitude," Anna Maria says. "I admire that."

I hold Barbie-Jackie tightly between my legs and pull off her hideously ugly head.

"Catch! Hot potato!" I yell at Anna Maria as I pitch the doll head her way.

"No, you're the hot potato!"

We toss Barbie-Jackie's head up and down, across the room, and flick it hard with a marble shooter, so that it skims across the hot-pink shag rug like a stone across a pond. I stick the head in my dungaree pocket and stash the headless body behind some doll boxes in my closet.

"Take a look at our hands," Anna Maria says.

Our palms and fingers are coated with pale pink, blue, green, and yellow from the Jordan almonds, dark brown from the shoe polish, and bright orange from the ballpoint pen. A car horn toots from the driveway.

"That's my mother," Anna Maria says. "Gotta go. Are you sure you're going to be okay?"

"Never felt better."

"Keep the last two pillboxes of Jordan almonds," Anna Maria says as she puts them under my pillow. "Make a wish before you fall asleep. Who knows? Maybe in the morning there'll be a brand-new, clean Barbie doll head under the pillow."

I walk Anna Maria to the door and wave hello to Mrs. Tucci. Then I take the Hoover out of the front hall closet. I vacuum my hot-pink shag rugs to get rid of the pieces of *matzoh* and doll hair. After I put it away, I lie down on my bed. I reach under my pillow for the Jordan almonds and polish them off. What's the point of waiting? I know it's going to take a lot more than a wish and sleeping on candy to make a new doll head magically appear in the morning. It's going to take a miracle like the parting of the Red Sea.

30

Happy Mother's Day, Mrs. K. I'm a Poet, Don't I Know It! My Feet Are Longfellows

ABIGAIL LEAH SHAPIRO

May 1, 1960

Dear Jackie,

Mother's Day is coming up. I've been making cards for Mummy and for Auntie Rina. I also drew some pictures to hang on the upstairs and downstairs refrigerators.

Last night I had a dream that Senator Kennedy won the election and you were busy making a list of who to invite to the inauguration. Guess what! Mummy and Auntie Rina were on the list. Mummy was invited because she's the hardest-working volunteer for the Kennedy campaign. She got to take one guest, and I told her to take Auntie Rina because she never gets to go anywhere, because all she does is take care of the family. I was frantic because

they needed me to design very special
dresses for them to wear. But naturally,
Abilea Coutures came through with
flying colors. I thought I'd show them
to you.

Bye!
Your Friend in Fashion,
Abby

P.S. Since the only chance that Mummy
would ever have of being invited to an
inauguration is when pigs fly, you don't
have to worry that these dresses will
go to waste. They can always wear them
for my Bat Mitzvah, whenever that will
be. Marty had his Bar Mitzvah when he
turned thirteen, but a girl can have a Bat
Mitzvah any time after the age of twelve.
I go to Sunday school and have Hebrew
instruction during the week. I want to
have a Bat Mitzvah even though Mummy says
she's not sure if it's necessary for girls.
She says that in the Old Country girls
didn't have such things. Then I remind her
for the millionth time that she was born
here and we don't have to do everything the
way it was in the Old Country. The problem
is that Mummy never makes any decisions
without first consulting Auntie Rina.
She's the boss of the whole family. If
Auntie Rina and Mummy look a little

sleepy in their sketches, it's because I was half-asleep when I drew them. I woke up from a dream, remember?

P.P.S. Happy Mother's Day, Jackie. I hope it's neat. Here are some new slippers to warm your feet.

I just wrote that poem to go with your new bathrobe and fuzzy slippers. I have the same pair. Anna Maria gave them to me for my last birthday. Mine are hot pink. Yours should be blue because the bathrobe is red, white, and blue. It's a patriotic bathrobe.

P.P.P.S. You don't look pregnant in the bathrobe. I did that on purpose so that it wouldn't be a maternity bathrobe. This way you can still wear it after your baby is born. I did put in pockets for holding the baby's bottle.

P.P.P.P.S. What do they serve at inaugurations, anyway? Do they have little finger foods like potato knishes and mini hot dogs wrapped up in puff-pastry blankets? We had those for Marty's Bar Mitzvah. I thought they were very tasty. Mummy wasn't happy with the caterer. She thought the hors d'oeuvres were a little greasy.

P.P.P.P.P.S. I had an interesting experience trying to turn my Barbie doll into a Jackie Kennedy doll. It was kind of like an operation. It didn't go too well. The patient died.

31
Maaaaaaarty's Baaaaaaack!

The door to the Pink Palace flings wide open. Marty is standing there in the doorway with his hands on his hips. He looks really mad. If this was a cartoon, steam would be blowing out of his ears and his eyes would be shooting arrows.

"Have you been in my bedroom without permission?" Marty demands.

"No. As you can see perfectly well with your own two brown eyes, I'm right here, right now, in my bedroom, which you just entered without knocking."

"I'm not talking about right now. I'm talking about anytime in the last few weeks."

"I don't know. Maybe," I say. "I can't remember."

Marty slams the bedroom door behind him and steps farther into the Pink Palace.

"Think hard, and you better give me the right answer, or else."

"Listen here, Maaaaaaarty," I say. "You can't just barge in here and start threatening me. I don't like it."

Marty moves in closer to my bed, where I am reclining and reading a *Highlights* magazine, a *Seventeen*, and a *National Geographic* with pictures of the aurora borealis.

"What did you just call me?" my brother asks.

This is the first time Marty has been in my bedroom in months. This is also the first time in months he's spoken more than two words to me.

"I bleated out your name. Maaaaaaarty. Because you look like a sheep with your hair all grown out and woolly-looking and your lips pressed together and your nostrils flaired and twitching around the way they are. You look like a sheep. You smell bad like a sheep. There are flies buzzing all around you. Want some grass to chew, Maaaaaaaarty?"

"You were in my room, I knew it!" he says. "Where's my whiffle stick. I need it. I'm going for a haircut today."

Ooops. I completely forgot about borrowing the whiffle stick. I really did. I meant to replace it but it slipped my mind just like that vinyl doll hair slipped off of Barbie-Jackie's whiffle stick–greased-up head.

"Okay, you just jogged my memory. There was an emergency and I had to use it," I say.

"That's it, Abby." Marty says. "I warned you to stay out of my room and away from my stuff. That was my spare tube for camp."

"I'll buy you another one," I say. "How much does it cost, Maaaaaaaarty?"

He lunges toward me and he's got that look in his eye. Not the look like he's going to cream me, but a different look. It's one I've seen loads of times. It's one that reminds me of the old Marty. I roll off the bed and grab the bedspread.

"*Toro, toro, olé, olé!* Back off, Mr. Bull. It is I, Abby, world-famous matador. Is Mr. Bull angry about his whiffle stick? Is Mr. Bull going to charge?"

I snort and stomp my foot. Marty yanks the bedspread from me and pulls me down onto the hot-pink shag rug. He pins down my arms and legs.

"I thought you said I was a sheep. How can I be a bull?"

"You are both," I say. "Half sheep, half bull, by the name of Maaaaaaarty."

"Okay, now you're going to get it! Bombs away," Marty says as he clear his throat to form a monster-sized spitball, which he will dangle within inches of my face.

"Wait, wait, don't do it. Let me show you for just one second why I needed your whiffle stickle. Please?"

Marty backs off and I reach into the bottom drawer of my desk, where the head of Barbie-Jackie has been living. I grip it and wind up a Ponytails pitch and let Marty have it. He squeals like a girl and falls backward onto the hot-pink shag rug. The blob of spit he was saving for me is now all over the front of his shirt.

"What is that? A shrunken head?"

"Yes, that's exactly what it is. A shrunken head from a tribe of cannibals. Go on, give it a little kiss," I say as I pick up Barbie-Jackie's head from the floor. "Shrunken head wants a kiss from Maaaaaaaarty."

Marty swipes the doll head from my hand and studies my handiwork.

"Oh man, Abby, you've gone and done it this time," Marty says.

"Yup. I done it good," I say.

"What were you trying to do to her?"

"It's a long story."

"I told Mum I'd take out the trash. Want me to pitch it?"

"Yuh. That's a good idea. Thanks, Maaaaaaaarty," I say.

My brother gives me a look.

"That was the last time I'll call you by your sheep name," I say. "I promise, Maaaaaaaarty."

Marty picks up Barbie-Jackie's head by the hair, which is held in place quite nicely by Anna Maria's excellent stapling job. He opens the door to the Pink Palace and takes one step out into the hallway.

"Marty?"

"What?"

"Is everything okay now between us?" I ask.

"Everything's okay," he answers. "Just as long as you don't ever ask me to buy you a bra."

"Marty?"

"Now what?"

"Come here. Please?"

Marty lays Barbie-Jackie's head down on my bureau and sits next to me on my bed. He puts his arms around me and gives me a hug. I drop my head onto his shoulder. My big brother is back.

32

"So Long, Farewell, Auf Wiedersehen, Good-Bye"

ABIGAIL LEAH SHAPIRO

July 22, 1960

Dear Jackie,

I won't take up much of your time. I know you are busy with the campaign and with being pregnant.

Here are two inaugural gowns for you. I'm sending them now that it's official that Senator Kennedy is the Democratic candidate. I know all about the nomination business because Mummy took me to a celebration party at headquarters. My brother, Marty, would have come, too, only he's away at Boy Scout sleepaway camp for the whole summer.

I know the election is not until November, but I'm sending you the sketches ahead of time. Here's why. Number one. I have always believed that Senator Kennedy will be our thirty-fifth president, so I'm

counting my chickens before they're hatched.
Number two. I'm done with you, Jackie
Kennedy. We're finished, kaput, end of the
line, finito! After today you will never
ever again receive any more sketches from
Abilea Coutures or any letters from me.

I design clothes that I think are
perfect for you, and I wait and wait for an
answer that never comes. What do you think?
That this is all so easy? That I just pop
off these letters? Well, it's not easy. It
takes a long time and a lot of brainpower
to sketch and to write these letters with
good penmanship. Sometimes I skip my
favorite television shows for you.

Okay, maybe at first it was fun. You
know, hoping to hear back from you. But
that was way back in October 1959, when
I was trying to earn money for a Barbie
doll. And then I couldn't stop writing to
you, even though I caught on pretty quick
that you would never answer my letters.
So I pretended that you were so excited
every time you opened one of my letters
because you couldn't wait to see what I had
designed for you.

This hasn't been a great year for me
as you know. Writing to you became as bad
a habit as chewing my cuticles. But you
know what, Jackie? If you try hard enough,
you can break bad habits. I don't chew my
cuticles anymore and I'm not going to write

to you anymore, either. Writing letters to you isn't much different than if I wrote letters to my father. My brother, Marty, called our father the Invisible Man. But I'm the Invisible Girl to you.

So go ahead, enjoy the gowns. I always wanted to be the one to design your inaugural gowns. And Abigail Leah Shapiro is no quitter. I am a pro. So here they are. I mostly like the one with the silk overblouse. I screwed up drawing your hands. I'm no good at hands. Anyway, the dress is a sleeveless sheath underneath the blouse. Peach would be a dreamy shade for this design. The second gown is ivory and has a million pearly beads all over the bodice, like the shimmery stuff they use to make the faces of watches. So wear all the new clothes in good health. Have fun in the White House because you, Jackie, are the Probable Future First Lady of the United States of America. I say this to you because I was brought up with manners, unlike some person who shall remain nameless.

Bye Forever,
Abigail Leah Shapiro
President and Chief Fashion Designer,
Abilea Coutures

P.S. Sixth grade turned out to be a year full of secrets and lies, and all I got out

191

of it was bupkes, "nothing." No mail and a
doll with no head.

P.P.S. Just out of curiosity, why didn't
you ever answer me? Was it because you
hated my designs? Was it because you were
insulted that some kid like me had the
chutzpa to charge you money?

P.P.P.S. This is the very last and final
thing. You must have gotten my letters.
Anna Maria Tucci's father works for
the post office, and he said if they
were undeliverable, they would have been
returned to sender. I never got any letters
returned.

P.P.P.P.S. I am truly disappointed that
you couldn't even write two measly lines
to me.

33
Wishful Thinking

"Look at this," Auntie Rina says, pointing to an article in *Life* magazine. "It says here: 'The candidate's striking wife, Jackie, who sticks close to her husband, has attracted almost as much attention as he has. Women crane to see what she is wearing.' Well, we know that to be the truth, don't we, Abby?"

It's a muggy Sunday July morning. We're lying on top of the covers instead of under the covers. We're wearing matching baby-doll pajamas.

"I don't care, really. I mean I hope Senator Kennedy wins the election, but I don't care about her anymore," I say.

"What's this I'm hearing? No more fashion design?"

"I still want to be a fashion designer, but not for her. Jackie Kennedy bores me."

"Oh, I see. Does this have to do with the fact that you never received any letters back from her?" Auntie Rina asks.

"No, not really," I fib. "I'm just taking a little vacation from sketching for a while."

"Well, if you're not interested in discussing fashion today, what do you want to talk about?"

I link my arm through Auntie Rina's and pull her close, even though it's a little too hot to be touching.

"I want to talk about dolls."

"One of our favorite subjects," Auntie Rina says.

"I know that you never had a doll when you were little. And I know all about the Gypsy woman's fortune and what happened to your foot. But there's got to be more to the story. Even if it's a really sad story, I'd still like to know. Don't leave out any important details. Okay?"

"Okay. But it's a long story, so let me first wet my whistle," she says, reaching over for the glass of water on her night table. "I'm like a desert, so parched. Want a sip?"

"No thanks."

Auntie Rina takes a deep breath and pauses for a few moments to collect her thoughts. "I told you that we left Vilna right after my father was buried. It was terrible for the obvious reasons, but also because we weren't able to sit *shiva* for him in the proper way."

I know all about sitting *shiva* because we did it in our house when my *Bubbie* Lena died. I was in third grade and it was the first time I'd ever been to a funeral. I didn't like it and I hope I never have to go to another one again. For seven days people came to our house to pay their respects to our family. They brought pastries and fruit and Mummy had the coffee percolator running nonstop. Auntie Rina made hard-boiled eggs and served bagels. She said that it's a custom to serve foods in those shapes because they represent the circle and cycle of life. All of the mirrors in the house were covered with sheets. Auntie Rina explained that when you mourn someone who has died, you should not be concerned with how you look. She didn't wear her red lipstick that entire week. But she also said that some people covered mirrors for another reason. They believed that if you looked into a mirror during *shiva*, you would see the angel of death staring right back at you. I wish she hadn't told me that. It gave me nightmares.

"Do you remember when *Bubbie* Lena died and Rabbi Levine

gave me, Mummy, Uncle Morris, and Uncle Max pins of black ribbon?"

"Uh-huh. I remember that the rabbi ripped them," I say.

"Tearing the black ribbon symbolizes that your heart is torn when somebody you love dies. In the Old Country mourners would actually tear their clothing. Well, *Bubbie* Lena was in such a state of grief on that passage to America that she sat and cried and ripped her shawl until it was nothing but a pile of shredded rags. I needed comfort, too. I loved my father. So I took the strips of cloth and made a lumpy rag doll. It wasn't much to look at, but I took great comfort in the doll. In my mind it was a way to hold on to a piece of my father. But the passage was two weeks long and rough, and everyone was sick. We were in steerage but were allowed to go to an upper deck to get some fresh air. And as I stood near the ship's railing, the rag doll slipped out of my hands and went overboard," Auntie Rina says.

"Oh no! What did you do?"

"There was nothing I could do but watch the doll bob up and down with the waves. For the rest of the voyage I wondered if the waves would carry the rag doll back to Europe or if she'd be waiting for me when we arrived in America."

"I know this is a silly question, but did the doll wash up on shore?"

"That would have been nice, wouldn't it? To have the doll waiting for me in America? That is child's fantasy, wishful thinking, just like what happened later on when that Gypsy woman told me that I'd find a real doll. This pain in my right foot has been a constant reminder my whole life of how foolish it is to wish for things that are not meant to be."

I slip my arm out of our hold and move to the end of the bed.

"You were right," I say.

"About what?"

"About Jackie. Maybe for me it was just child's fantasy, too, like you said. Wishful thinking that she'd write back to me."

"Maybe, or maybe there are many valid reasons why she never wrote back. You just don't know what they are. People always think the worst when they don't have the correct information."

"My father said he knew why she'd never answer me. He told me that Mummy did, too."

"When did your father say that?"

"The night before he left."

"Your father was neither happy nor kind. He was just playing with you for his own amusement, like a cat batting a mouse. *Farshteyst*? 'Understand?'"

I nod.

"Your father was being cruel, that's all. He took his frustrations over his relationship with your mother out on you. But he's gone now, so you must let go of what he said."

"Okay, Auntie Rina," I say. "I'll try."

I close my eyes and try to make the memory of that night slip away just like Auntie Rina's rag doll in the Atlantic Ocean. But it doesn't work. The memory isn't like the rag doll. It doesn't drown in the ocean. It just keeps riding the waves and rolling back to me.

34
White Lies Don't Really Count

Mrs. Whelan is at the front door.

"Hi, Abby. Nice to see you," she says. "Is your mother home?"

"It's good to see you, too. Come on in. Let me go get her."

"No, that's okay. I'll wait out here."

Mrs. Whelan looks even thinner than usual. But she looks nice in a white sailor blouse with blue piping and matching blue denim culottes. This is the first time I've seen her hair down, and not all knotted in a French twist. This new way is soft and pretty, set in a flip. She's been gone from the neighborhood since that night when the ambulance took her away four months ago.

I leave the front screen door open and run to the basement to get Mummy. She's doing laundry down there.

"Gladys, won't you come in?" my mother asks, a little breathless from rushing up the stairs.

"No thanks, Betty. Abby already asked. I just wanted to come by and tell you in person how much I appreciated what you and the other neighbors did for me."

The women on Darlene Avenue cleaned Mrs. Whelan's house and filled the refrigerator with fresh food before she was discharged from the hospital. She was in a special place, not exactly a hospital and not exactly a mental institution. It was someplace where she had to dry out once and for all and get rid of the demons that made her do what she did to herself on that March night.

"Oh, Gladys, there's no need for thank-you. That's what neighbors do for each other," Mummy says. "You're looking well-rested."

"Yes, I am. I feel this time I'm on the road to recovery for real," Mrs. Whelan says.

"I'm sure you are," Mummy says.

There is a little bit of an awkward silence. Mummy looks like she's anxious to get back to the basement and finish the laundry.

"One other thing, Betty," Mrs. Whelan says. "I wanted to invite Abby to a party."

"Party?"

"Well, it's more of a family reunion. Down the Cape this coming Sunday. At Onset Beach. My cousin's daughter, Adele, will be there. She's about Abby's age. And there'll be plenty of other children there as well."

It sounds like fun to me. This summer has been a bomb except for the few weeks I went to day camp. Marty's been in New Hampshire at Boy Scout sleepaway camp and Anna Maria's been on the Jersey shore with her cousins for the past month.

"We're going to have a real, old-fashioned New England clambake," Mrs. Whelan says.

"What's a clambake? Something to do with clams?" I ask.

"Why it's just about the best thing in the whole world," Mrs. Whelan says with a lot more excitement in her voice than when she first rang the doorbell. "We build a fire pit on the beach and cook lobsters, crabs, mussels, right there in the sand."

"And clams. Don't forget about the clams."

Mrs. Whelan smiles.

"Yes, Abby, and clams."

"Wow, it sounds like a blast. I love lobster and crab and all that stuff."

I turn to Mummy. She puts her arm around my shoulder and squeezes me tight.

"That is so thoughtful of you, Gladys. But I'm afraid it's entirely out of the question."

Mrs. Whelan's face drops.

"Betty, if you're worried that I…you have my word. I would never…," she says in a hushed voice.

"Of course not, Gladys," Mummy says. "That never crossed my mind. I know you would never drink and drive. Especially with a child in the car. It's just that we have a prior commitment."

"I understand," Mrs. Whelan says. "Next time, perhaps."

"Yes, Gladys. Next time," Mummy says.

My mother about-faces and goes back down to the basement. I watch Mrs. Whelan cross the street and walk up her driveway. Before she goes inside her house, she turns around and sees me still standing at the screen door. I wave. She waves back, then disappears inside her house.

I bound down the basement stairs two at a time. Mummy doesn't hear me walk into the laundry room. She's filling the washing machine with soap powder for another load. The dryer is making a clanging noise from open dungaree zippers and loose change that spins around in the drum.

"Why do you hate her? What did she ever do to you?" I demand.

Mummy closes the lid to the washing machine to lower the volume of noise in the room.

"I don't hate her. I don't hate anybody," she says. "Not even your father. Hate gets you nowhere fast."

"But you don't like her, do you?"

My mother wets her lips before she speaks.

"Gladys Whelan is not my cup of tea."

"You were very rude to her," I say. "If she starts drinking again, it'll be your fault."

"First of all, I wasn't rude. I was direct. There's a difference. And second, if Gladys starts drinking again, it'll be her own fault. She's in charge of herself, not me."

"You lied to her. Why did you do that?"

"I told a little white lie. White lies don't really count. I didn't want to tell her the truth that she's not out of the hospital long enough to have the responsibility of driving you back and forth to the Cape. How do I know if I can trust her? And since when are you such a shellfish *maven*?" Mummy asks, using the Yiddish word for "expert." "Lobster, crab? You've never eaten those things, have you?"

"No. I just said that. I was excited. I really wanted to go."

"Oh. Are you sure you're not telling a white lie?" Mummy asks. "Maybe you have eaten those foods or done lots of other things behind my back. How would I know?"

"Are you asking me or accusing me? Because it sure sounds like you're accusing me."

"Abby, I'm not accusing you of anything."

"Did you like the blouse Mrs. Whelan was wearing?" I ask. "That sailor blouse?"

"It was nice. Why are you asking me about her clothes? I thought we were talking about shellfish."

"Would you ever wear something like that? Is that your taste?" I ask.

"No, never. What's gotten into you today? I'd like to get this laundry done before supper," Mummy says.

"Even when you were a lot younger, you'd never wear anything like that?"

"No. I have never worn anything in that style. Are we finished here?"

"Yuh. We're finished," I say.

I leave her there in the laundry room with the smell of the detergent and bleach and the washing machine and dryer playing a duet of sounds. I walk past the cedar closet. The door is open. I don't want to go in the cedar closet ever again. But if I don't, I'll never get that photograph of Auntie Rina and Mummy in their sailor dresses.

Today there's no Marty to help me. So I pile several boxes on top of each other and step up, hoping that the boxes won't collapse under my weight. I stretch my right arm high and sweep across the top shelf with a heavy wooden coat hanger. The shoebox of photographs falls down, along with a pair of baby shoes and a brown-paper lunch bag. I rummage through the lot of photographs until I find the one I want. I wind up my pitching arm and hurl the baby shoes back up to the shelf. Good landing. The brown-paper lunch bag is filled with papers. I fold down the top to the bag and toss it up as well. Only I miss my mark. The lunch bag topples down, emptying its rubber-banded contents at my feet. Stuffed in between bank statements, coupons, and postcards are ten pink envelopes addressed to Mrs. Jacqueline Kennedy, with my name and return address printed in bold black letters on the back. The seal I made with gold wax and an embosser is broken on every single envelope.

35

The Jigsaw Puzzle of Our Lives

It's dark by the time I decide to go home. The woods were the only place I could think of to escape to where I'd be completely alone. I would stay there forever except that the mosquitoes are eating me up alive. Or maybe it's poison ivy. Or both. I can't tell. I itch all over and my eyelids feel heavy. I crawled under a thicket of bushes and vines, where I lay down on the ground the whole time. It was sometime after lunch when I ran out of the house. Maybe it was one o'clock. I fell asleep for a long while. Now I can see the Big Dipper in the night sky.

I didn't bother to reread the ten letters I'd written to Jackie. What for? I knew what was in them. It was me who wrote every single word. It was me who carefully sealed the envelopes with gold sealing wax which I'd saved for a special occasion. I don't care anymore that my mother knows the details about all the secrets I've collected, but how dare she! How could she do this to me? How could she steal my letters and read my private property? Why didn't she throw them out in the trash? Why did she hide them away, thinking they'd never be found in a million years? It makes me sick to my stomach knowing that my father was telling the truth.

Every light in the house is burning bright. Upstairs and

downstairs. As I head up Darlene Avenue I see Mummy, Auntie Rina, and Uncle Morris pacing back and forth on the driveway. They each hold a flashlight in their hands.

"Oh my God, where have you been?" Mummy cries when she sees me.

Her flashlight crashes down onto the driveway. It rolls to my feet. I do not pick it up.

"You're covered in dirt! Look at your fingers! Did somebody take you? Were you kidnapped? Are you all right? Tell us what happened! We've been frantic with worry. We called the police to report you missing."

My mother squeezes me tight and kisses me all over my face and head. She's crying. I don't care. I do not feel sorry for her. My heart is as cold as stone. I stand stiffly, with my arms hanging by my side. I imagine I'm protected in a metal space suit, like the alien coming out of the flying saucer in the movie *The Day the Earth Stood Still*. It could be army soldiers' bullets shooting at me. Doesn't matter. Nothing is going to penetrate my shield.

"Oh, Abby, I was petrified when I couldn't find you. All I could think about was that little Myerson boy."

My mother is talking about a child who used to live about a half mile away from us. One day he went into his backyard to play and was never seen again. His family searched for years until the police found his skeleton in a trunk in an abandoned building.

"Get your hands off me," I bark at my mother. "Now!"

My mother steps back and blinks hard.

"Abby, what's going on?" Auntie Rina asks. "No, wait! First just tell me that you're okay."

"Yuh. I'm okay, except for her. I don't ever want to talk to her again. And I mean it!" I shout.

I emphasize the word "her" louder than the other words.

"Abby, what's wrong?" Mummy asks.

She looks confused. Like she actually doesn't know what I'm talking about.

"Shut up! You're nothing but a liar!"

Mummy says nothing. She's in shock. Auntie Rina steps up to the plate and takes charge like she always does.

"Morris, could you excuse us for a few moments?" she says. "We need a little private time here. And call the police right away to tell them Abby's been found. Please."

Auntie Rina always knows the right thing to do. Uncle Morris is looking a bit uncomfortable. He picks up the fallen flashlight, then starts to walk up the driveway. He stops and turns around.

"I'm glad you're safe and sound, Abby," he says to me. "That's the only thing that counts."

Then he continues up the driveway and into the house.

No, Uncle Morris. You're wrong. That's not the only thing that counts.

"Go on," I shout at my mother. "Tell your sister what you did!"

"Abby, please lower your voice," Mummy says. "We're outside. The whole neighborhood can hear you shouting. Voices carry at night. Especially in the summer."

"Good! Then let them all hear the truth that you stink as a mother," I say.

Mummy looks to Auntie Rina and shrugs her shoulders.

"I swear, I don't know what this is all about. Did you run away because I said you couldn't go to the Cape with Mrs. Whelan?" Mummy asks. "Is that it? All I know is that one minute you're in the laundry room and then I couldn't find you anywhere. I was... we all were worried sick that God forbid, *keynehore* poo poo poo"— my mother spits three times over her left shoulder—"something awful happened."

"Something awful did happen to me. I got you for a mother. And stop with that stupid spitting and your stupid rules and sins and your stupid superstitions. I'm sick of them and I'm sick of you."

"Okay, that's enough," Auntie Rina says like a boxing referee.

She grabs my hand and drags me onto the porch. She points to the divan.

"Sit," she commands. "And please speak calmly."

Then she drags a chair across the porch.

"And Betty, you stay right over here."

There's a moment of quiet, except for the chirping of the backyard crickets. Auntie Rina stands in between us.

"Listen, Abby. If nobody bothered you, touched you, or hurt you, then I don't need to know where you've been all these hours." Auntie Rina says. "But I do need to know why you're so angry at your mother."

"You want to know? I'll tell you," I say.

I'm all worked up and I'm breathing fast and hard. My chest is rising up and down. My eyes feel like they're burning. I rub them anyway with the filthy palms of my filthy hands.

"You want to know why I never heard back from Jackie Kennedy? The reason is because she never got any of my letters."

"What are you saying?" Auntie Rina asks.

"She never mailed them."

I point to my mother like Perry Mason does to the guilty person in the courtroom every week.

"Not even one letter. I'm talking all the way back to October 1959. That's almost a year. She opened them, read them, and hid them so I'd never find out."

I wiggle my shoulder blades back and forth across the seams on the plastic upholstery. I'm dying from the itching.

Auntie Rina looks at my mother with very sad eyes.

"Betty, is this true?"

My mother taps her foot on the stone porch floor.

"Oh, for heaven's sake. She wanted to charge Jacqueline Kennedy money. Can you imagine? It's one thing to send her drawings, but to sell them? To ask for money? I felt an obligation as a mother not to let those letters go out."

"Do not change the facts," Auntie Rina says angrily. "You should never have known what was in those letters. Your obligation as a mother was to mail them. Plain and simple!"

"Auntie Rina, I only asked Jackie Kennedy for money in the beginning and it wasn't for much. It was a tiny amount of money. Pennies, practically. I just wanted to show her I was a hardworking kid trying to save for a Barbie doll, that's all," I say.

"Oh, Barbie? That's *noch a mayse*, 'another story,'" my mother says. "The doll with the big bosoms. Can you believe this child had the audacity to ask Jacqueline Kennedy, one of the most famous women in the country, how old she was when she got her first bra?"

Auntie Rina takes a seat next to me on the divan. She slowly shakes her head.

"Maybe Abby needed a mother to talk to. You haven't exactly been present. You were either wrapped up in your own misery or so proud of yourself in your new life as an activist for Negroes. Oh, and let's not forget the countless hours you put in for the Kennedy campaign. With you, Betty, it's feast or famine. You're either walking around slobby or dressed up like you're going to the theater. You're either down in the dumps or up on cloud nine."

"Oh, now you're criticizing me for being involved in worthy causes? I need purpose in my life." Mummy says. "I've gone too many years without it."

"Being involved with causes is a good thing, but not if you ignore your daughter's needs," Auntie Rina says. "Shame on you! You don't know how lucky you are to have such wonderful children. They should be the primary purpose in your life. I'm sorry to say that you've been a selfish mother."

"How dare you! You have no right to talk to me like that!"

Auntie Rina ignores what Mummy says and turns to me.

"Abby, where are the letters?" she asks.

"I got rid of them," I tell her.

"That's good," Mummy says. "The things she wrote about this family! The way she described Max, you'd think he was the mobster Bugsy Siegel. And me, I'm the Wicked Witch of the West. But you, Rina, everything you say is golden. Abby quotes you like the Bible."

"I can't believe what I'm hearing," Auntie Rina says.

"Believe it. And the secrets that Abby kept. You can't begin to imagine what she kept from us."

"That's not the point, Betty. I can't believe that a mother would break her daughter's trust."

"I did it to protect her. Jackie Kennedy would never have answered a child's letters. And she never would have sent her money for the fashion designs. Admit it, I saved Abby a lot of heartbreak," Mummy says.

"You caused her a lot of heartbreak," Auntie Rina says.

"For your information I could have taken the rejection," I say to my mother. "But you took away my chance of ever getting any kind of a letter from Jackie."

And then it hits me big. My stomach feels like I just went on a roller coaster for the first time. My mother read everything. She knows that my father beat me. I can't speak in a calm voice any more. I scream.

"You knew that my father hit me! You knew it, and you did nothing about it!"

"Oh my God," Auntie Rina cries. "Abby, I had no idea. You should have come to me."

I get up from the divan and stand right in front of my mother.

"You make me sick. You stood up for Effie. You stood up for Marty. You said nobody had the right to hurt your child. You sent Uncle Max and Sy to take care of his teacher. But what did you do for me? Did you send Uncle Max and Sy to International Falls, Minnesota, to take care of business? No, you did not. You probably figured I just got what was coming to me. Huh? Was that it? I don't mean anything to you!"

"Oh, Abby, that's not true. I nearly died when I read that part," my mother says in a soft voice. "But by that time it was too late."

"I will never forgive you. I hate you!"

"Abby, don't say that," Auntie Rina says. "You don't really mean that."

"Yes, I really do. I should have kept on running and never come back."

I'm so angry and so itchy. I feel like I'm on fire.

"Betty, you just don't get it," Auntie Rina says. "You had no right to interfere. I'm deeply ashamed of your behavior."

My mother gets up and stands in front of Auntie Rina. She puts her hands on her hips.

"Well, if it isn't the pot calling the kettle black. You're a fine one to talk. All you've ever done is interfere with my life. I never should have listened to you. I've wasted my life trying to please you. I never should have married Hank. What did I know about love? You just kept telling me I was getting older, and if I didn't hurry up, I'd never have children. And so what happened? I had children only for you and Morris to take them as your own."

"Somebody had to step in. You weren't doing a very good job half the time," Auntie Rina says.

"How dare you!" Mummy says.

"I never put a gun to your head. I didn't make you stay married. You had a choice," Auntie Rina says.

"And what about Max? He doesn't come around anymore. That's because of you. You drove him away. It would be nice to get to know my new sister-in-law," Mummy says. "Especially now that there's a baby on the way."

"I'm not stopping you," Aunt Rina answers.

"Oh, please."

Now it's their voices that are raised. They are shouting and finger-pointing. I'm sure every neighbor on the street and maybe one street over in both directions can hear them. Their argument has changed. It is no longer about me. I get up and pull the photograph of the two of them in their sailor dresses out of my back pocket. I rip it in half and then rip it in half again.

"Liar again," I say as I throw the photograph at my mother. "So you never in your whole life wore a sailor dress? No, make that three times a liar. Because I know you lied about the baby picture from Mrs. Whelan, too. Where did you hide that one? Never mind. I don't care. I'm going to take a shower and go to bed. But I'm not sleeping downstairs anymore. I don't want to be anywhere near you. I'm moving upstairs. Is that okay with you, Auntie Rina?" I ask.

"Yes. Go ahead. Take sheets from the linen closet."

My mother picks up the pieces of the photograph and slowly sinks down onto the divan. She holds them on her lap and fits them back together. Auntie Rina sits down next to her. She sighs as she sees the image of them in their sailor dresses.

"I haven't seen this in a million years."

"How young we looked," Mummy says.

"We *were* young," Auntie Rina answers.

They are no longer yelling at each other. They sit on the divan perfectly still and stare at the photograph. It reminds me of my fourth-grade field trip to the Museum of Fine Arts in Boston. We walked around with a guide who talked about all of the paintings. She pointed to brass plates on the walls that had the artist's name and the title of their painting. That's what Mummy and Auntie Rina look like—a museum painting. If I had to give their painting a title, I would call it. *Two Sisters Sitting on the Porch Putting Together the Jigsaw Puzzle of Their Lives.*

36
One of Those Meant-To-Be Things

The rest of August crept by. I stayed busy mostly reading, playing with my dolls, and listening to the radio. I learned all the words to "Itsy Bitsy Teeny Weeny Yellow Polka Dot Bikini." It seemed like the radio stations played that song every two minutes. The other song they played every five minutes was "The Twist." I practiced doing the dance that goes with the song by watching Chubby Checker on American Bandstand. I made up my mind to teach Marty the dance when he came home. I was sure he hadn't learned the Twist at Boy Scout camp. I'd have to be patient on account of Marty's two left feet.

There were some changes in the neighborhood. The family with the twins now have a new baby. Mrs. Lazarus died in her sleep. Now there's a for-sale sign on her front lawn. Mr. Lane is still an eligible bachelor. The only change in his life is that he bought a gasoline lawnmower. Mrs. Whelan has been keeping sober. She goes to a meeting every day to make sure it stays that way. And she got her old job back at the telephone company. The only thing that hasn't changed on Darlene Avenue is the sweeping. The sisters are still out there every day with their brooms.

I spent a lot of time watching television in Uncle Morris's bedroom. There were a lot of stories on the news about Senator Kennedy and Jackie on the road campaigning and at parties. She always looked so pretty. All I could think about was that she could have been wearing fashions from Abilea Coutures. There was other interesting news, too. Important news, like about all the protests and sit-ins at luncheonettes that wouldn't serve food to Negroes or made them sit in special sections. That made me hope even more that Senator Kennedy would win the election. I knew he would keep his promise about working hard for civil rights.

And then there was the satellite called Sputnik 5 that the Russians launched into space. I couldn't believe that on Sputnik 5 there were two dogs, Belka and Strelka, forty mice, and two rats. I was worried that the dogs wouldn't make it back safely to earth. But they did. I didn't care too much about the rodents.

It took me awhile to get used to sleeping in *Bubbie* Lena's old bed. The mattress was a lot harder than the one on my bed downstairs. And the Lavender Palace was hotter at night than the Pink Palace. Auntie Rina said that was on account of hot air rising, so the upstairs of the house would always be hotter than the downstairs. Some nights I had a lot of trouble falling asleep. But it wasn't from the heat or Auntie Rina's snoring. That was something I never knew about her. She could be just as loud as Uncle Morris next door.

Those nights when I couldn't sleep, all I could think about was what Mummy did to me. Auntie Rina could always tell by the sounds of my breathing that I was awake. That's when she'd take the opportunity to talk to me about forgiving my mother.

"Your mother's apologized to you countless times, Abby. If you continue on this path and not accept her apology, then things will never be right between the two of you," she said. "Just keep in mind that the High Holy Days are around the corner. I shouldn't have to remind you that it's the time of year for forgiveness."

Marty finally came home from camp. He loved it and said he wanted to go back next summer. He'd grown two inches and looked even taller with his whiffle haircut all grown out. His hair was back to where he started before he got his camp haircut. I rubbed Marty's head first thing when he stepped off the bus.

"Do you want to call me Maaaaaaarty?" he asked when I gave him a welcome-home hug.

Marty could tell right away that something was wrong. It was obvious that I wasn't speaking to Mummy, no matter how hard she tried to make conversation. I told Marty in private that maybe I could go to sleepaway camp next summer, but it would have to be a special place for girls with lying mothers. Marty felt very bad for me but said that the mess was between me and Mummy. He didn't have a beef with her. She hadn't done a terrible thing to him.

It was great when Anna Maria finally came home. She told me funny stories about all of her New Jersey cousins and how they teased her on account of her New England accent. She made me laugh with her impersonations of them with their New Jersey accents. Anna Maria said they called it New Joisey. She also told me that her New Jersey cousins were dying to swap Barbie doll clothes with her. They said her Barbie had the most beautiful outfits they'd ever seen in their whole lives.

A few days before school started, Mrs. Tucci took us into Boston to shop for back-to-school clothes at Jordan Marsh and Filene's Basement. Auntie Rina gave me the money to shop for myself. She said I was old enough to make my own decisions. But the real reason was because she knew I wouldn't go shopping with Mummy like we always did before school.

Mrs. Tucci decided that we would take the bus into Boston rather than drive. She sat in the seat in front of us reading the newspapers, and we sat behind her studying the map of West Junior High School. Even though we'd had a tour of the building before the end of sixth grade, we were still a little worried about getting lost. Marty told us not to sweat it. He was in ninth grade, so we were in the same building. He said he'd give us a special tour once school started.

"Oh my," Mrs. Tucci said as she folded back a page of the Boston daily paper.

"What, Ma, what?" Anna Maria asked.

Mrs. Tucci raised the newspaper so we could see.

"Well, here's a story about a man who was arrested by the FBI for embezzling money from the bank where he worked," she said.

"So?"

"His name is Terrence Grover Applegate. Isn't there a girl at your school with the last name of Applegate?" Mrs. Tucci asked.

"What?" we both said at the exact same time.

I punched Anna Maria in the shoulder.

"Owe me a Coke," I mouthed at her.

"It says here that he's in jail and will stay there until his trial because his family couldn't post bail. Hmmm," Mrs. Tucci said.

"What? What?" Anna Maria asked. "Don't read it to yourself. Tell us."

"The FBI had been watching him for a long time. They said it was only a matter of time before they caught him."

"Susie Applegate's father was the president of a bank," I said.

"Not according to the paper," Mrs. Tucci said. "The article says he worked for many years as a teller and for the last two years he was a loan officer."

"Oh wow," I said. "That's not what Susie told the class."

"You know what, Abby," Mrs. Tucci said. "Susie might not have known. Her father might have told the family another story. Some people lead double lives."

Susie never showed up at West Junior High for the first day of school. I figured the family must have moved away because of their troubles. Susie was not my favorite person in the world, but I felt very sorry for her. I knew exactly how she felt. My father lived a double life, too. To the outside world he was charming, the greatest thing since sliced bread. But to his family he was sullen and sarcastic. Susie's life was never going to be the same and it had nothing to do with her. What her father did wasn't her fault, but she'd be paying for it for a long time.

Then on Tuesday, September 8, just one week into school, two things happened. Susie Applegate walked into homeroom right at the eight o'clock bell. Anna Maria sits behind me and kicked the heels of my shoes. Susie looked terrible. She kept her eyes on the floor while everyone whispered and giggled behind her back. Me and Anna Maria said hello to her. Nobody else did.

The second thing that happened was that Auntie Rina was taken away by ambulance. A bunch of blood vessels in her brain burst. She was born with a weakness in her brain. There was no way to know about this ahead of time. But it was *bashert*, one of those "meant-to-be" things. Someday, somewhere, those blood vessels were going to burst. That weakness was there when she hid in the pickle barrel, when she lost her rag doll on the trip to America, when the horse cart ran over her foot, when the Gypsy woman told her a fortune, and all during those forty years when Sy tried to take her out on a date. The only warning she had was the terrible headache that came on just seconds before she fell. She walked out of the store to get some coffee and collapsed on the hard concrete sidewalk. Just like that.

37
No Slap in the Face

There have been no after-school activities for me, no twelfth-birthday celebration, no going to synagogue for the High Holy Days, no Hanukkah, nor much of anything else. All of my after-school and weekend time has been spent at the hospital and rehabilitation center.

Auntie Rina wasn't expected to live. Most people with this kind of brain injury don't even make it to the hospital alive. And if they do, they usually die during surgery or right afterward. It was touch and go for a long while. There were other complications, too. How she fell on the hard sidewalk fractured her skull, collarbone, an elbow, and an ankle. And then there was the brain swelling after the surgery to repair the blood vessels. The whole family sat in a pea-soup fog of fear in the intensive care waiting room praying and hoping for the best. All I could think of was that Rabbi Levine would be coming to our house to rip the black-ribbon mourning pins.

Uncle Max worked in the store so Uncle Morris could take a rest. Then Marty worked after school so Uncle Max could go back to the Pink Elephant. Aunt Dolores cooked food for us, even though her feet were swollen and her belly big from being pregnant. Mummy moved into the hospital. She brought a bag with a change of clothes and refused to leave even when the doctors strongly suggested that she go home. But Mummy wouldn't budge, so they finally gave in and let her sleep on the waiting-room couch.

Uncle Morris hired all of the part-time salesgirls to work full-time in the store. Flo, Kathleen, and Mary kept the business going. I told Uncle Morris to call Mrs. Applegate. I figured she could probably use a job. She accepted his offer and has worked out great. Turned out she's a natural for selling shoes and pocketbooks.

Mummy and I spent a lot of time together in the waiting room in between visiting hours. At first we didn't talk much. We just watched a lot of television. Then we started to talk about what we watched on television. We discussed the debates between Senator Kennedy and Vice President Nixon, the big ticker-tape parade for Kennedy in New York City, the election coverage, and the report about the Kennedy's new baby boy, named John Fitzgerald Kennedy, Jr.

"You were right, Abby," Mummy said out of the blue one afternoon.

"About what?"

"So many things. Not mailing the letters, of course. That goes without saying. I should have been a better mother to you and to Marty. That just eats away at my insides. You kids shouldn't have to pay for my mistakes."

I listened while she talked.

"It would be easy to say it was all your father's fault, that he made me so unhappy that I took it out on you," Mummy said.

"Like the dog kicks the cat and the cat kicks the mouse."

"Yes, but that's no excuse. I truly am sorry."

"Yuh, I know. You've said so a million times, like a broken record. But it doesn't really change what happened, does it?"

"No, it doesn't," Mummy said.

"And it doesn't change how I feel about you, either."

"I know," Mummy said. "And I only have myself to blame."

"What about the baby photograph of me with a pink ribbon?" I asked. "Did you lie about that, too?"

"Oh, Abby! One day when you were a few months old, I let *Bubbie* Lena walk you in the carriage. I should have followed behind, but I didn't. I stood in the driveway and watched. I told her to go to the end of the street and come back. I thought she would listen to me. But she didn't come back. I ran to the end of Darlene Avenue, and you were nowhere in either direction. I ran back up the street and pounded on the Whelans' door. Mr. ·Whelan hadn't left for work yet, so he called in other policemen and they searched for you. They found *Bubbie* Lena rocking you in a carriage in some stranger's backyard about two miles away. When he brought you and *Bubbie* back, he yelled at me for being an unfit mother. He said he had a good mind to cuff me and bring me down to the station house and arrest me. And then Gladys joined in and said I didn't deserve to have such a precious angel. I was humiliated in front of the whole neighborhood. Thank goodness Auntie Rina was at the store, and by some miracle she never found out what happened. But they were right. I was an unfit mother. I allowed your grandmother, who was already *oyverbotl*, to be in charge of you. I didn't use the best judgement. That seems to be a pattern with me," Mummy said.

"I don't know what that Yiddish word means," I said. "I never heard it before."

"It means that you're confused, senile."

"Oh," I said. "And did you throw away the picture?"

"No. It's boxed up somewhere in the basement."

"And the sailor dresses?"

"That was not a lie. It was so long ago, and truthfully, I forgot all about that day at the Cape."

"Okay."

"You know, it's not too late," Mummy said. "You could still send your designs to Jackie. You have the original sketches, don't you?"

"No, it is too late."

We sat quiet for a long while on the torn plastic couch in the hospital waiting room until it was time to see Auntie Rina.

"Why did you keep the letters? If you weren't going to mail them, why didn't you toss them in the garbage?" I asked. "I don't understand why you did that."

"I couldn't bring myself to do it. They were a part of you. I suppose it's the same reason why I couldn't throw away Mrs. Whelan's gift. And I was so proud of your designs. The outfits were beautiful. You showed so much talent," she said.

I looked away. "It's a little late for compliments, don't you think?"

"I know you're not a little girl anymore. I see that now."

"Yuh, okay, great."

"We never had the talk a mother and daughter should have about your body. How pretty soon things will happen to you."

"Forget it. I don't need you. I know all about it."

"Well, what you might not know is about a custom from the Old Country. It's something that mothers do to their daughters when it happens for the first time," Mummy said.

"And?" I asked.

"They give their daughters a smack across the face."

"That's so stupid," I said.

"Well, they don't hit them that hard. It's meant to be a symbol of womanhood, to put some color back in their cheeks," Mummy said. "Or some other foolish nonsense. And yes, it is a very stupid custom."

"You aren't planning on doing that to me, are you?" I asked Mummy. "Because I'm telling you right now that I won't let you."

"I think that's one tradition from the Old Country that can stay in the Old Country," Mummy said.

The nurse comes into the waiting area and tells us we can go in now to see Auntie Rina. My mother smiles at me. I do not smile back. I know she's sorry, but that's not enough to make the hurt go away.

"You know, Abby, I don't expect you to believe me, but the two happiest days of my life were when you and Marty were born."

I do not answer. I just keep walking ahead of my mother down the hallway to Auntie Rina.

38
There's No Place Like Home

There must be two feet or more of snow on the ground. The channel four meteorologist warned that we'd get a giant nor'easter, and for once he was right on the money. It stopped snowing before dawn, but the wind keeps on swirling snow all over the place. The drifts look like Cape Cod sand dunes.

The plows came down Darlene Avenue twice. Marty built up his arm muscles pushing the snowblower down the driveway. I did my share by shoveling out the walkway to the front door. It took me two hours to do the job. I was cold, wet, and very sore by the time I came indoors. But that's okay because I am very happy today.

Auntie Rina came home from the rehabilitation center a few days ago. She still tires easily and will have to rest a lot. A special nurse will come to the house to help her with her exercises. But her doctors promised that by spring she'd be as fit as a fiddle.

Mummy got her settled in her bedroom. I took at least a dozen dolls from my collection and placed them all around her in bed.

"Here are some friends to keep you company," I told her. "You always said that if you didn't have to go to work, you'd play with dolls for hours. Here's your big chance!"

"Thank you, Abby," Auntie Rina said.

"You're very welcome," I told her.

"Come closer, sweetie pie," she said while she held out her arms to hug me. "Remember the story I told you about the Gypsy woman and my fortune?"

"Of course I remember. She told you that someday you'd find a real doll of your own," I said.

"When I told you that story, I should have ended it in a different way. I should have told you that my fortune finally came true the day your parents brought you home from the hospital. I knew the moment I held you in my arms that the Gypsy woman's words came true. Now don't go running to Marty to tattle that I love you more than him, because that's not what I'm saying. I love you both the same, only you are my little doll and always will be."

"I love you, too, Auntie Rina," I said.

We hugged and sniffled for a long minute or two.

"Okay, enough of this mushy stuff. Now play with the dolls. That's Dr. Abigail's prescription," I ordered.

Today is Friday, January 20, 1961, and the inauguration of Senator John Fitzgerald Kennedy. He will be sworn in as the thirty-fifth president of the United States of America. Washington, DC, was hit hard with snow, too. It was reported on the television news that the army was called in to clear up the mess. They had to use flamethrowers to melt the snow. But everything looks just fine now as we watch the motorcade come down Pennsylvania Avenue.

My whole family is gathered in the downstairs den. Me, Auntie Rina, Mummy, Marty, and Uncle Morris. The store will stay closed because of the weather. Uncle Morris says he doubts any of the stores on the main street will be open for business today. Mummy set up a card table with snacks and ginger ale. We have everything we need to be comfortable when we watch the inauguration.

"Was that the doorbell?" Auntie Rina asks. "What kind of a *meshuggener* would come out in this weather?"

I know who it is. I am the one who arranged for this "crazy person" to drive through snowy and slippery streets to get here.

"I'll get it," Mummy says.

"We'll come with you, too," Uncle Morris and Marty say.

I have to move quickly. I reach into my pocket, where I've hidden Auntie Rina's tube of red lipstick. She hasn't worn any since she was taken to the hospital.

"An important person once told me that all you need in this life are kind thoughts, a genuine smile, and the perfect shade of red lipstick. That's guaranteed to make you look and feel like a million bucks. Now pucker up while I make you more beautiful than you already are."

"Oh, Abby, what have you done!" she says as I color her lips.

"Now blot," I say, holding a clean white handkerchief in between her lips. "Just one more thing. This important person I'm talking about also said that in this life you need to give people the benefit of the doubt."

"Rina, you've got company," Mummy sings out in a very cheery voice.

Sy walks into the den holding a bouquet of yellow roses. I am impressed. I suppose only someone with connections could get them during a blizzard. Sy says hello to each of us and offers the roses to Auntie Rina. Sy hasn't seen Auntie Rina in a very long time. Only immediate family members were allowed to visit her in the hospital.

"They're lovely, Sy. Thank you," she says.

I know that Auntie Rina is pleased to see Sy. I can tell because she smiles and her hazel eyes are crinkled up, so only a little bit of them shine through.

"How are you feeling, Rina?" Sy asks.

"Can't complain," she says.

We leave Auntie Rina and Sy alone in the den. One by one we quietly go up the front staircase and watch the inauguration in

Uncle Morris's bedroom. Jackie looks nice and happy. She's wearing a simple wool coat with fur trim around the collar and has a fur muffler to keep her hands warm. I have to laugh, though, because she's got another one of those pillbox hats on her head. I'm the one who really deserves credit for that new fashion trend. I bet anything Anna Maria is thinking the exact same thing as she watches the inauguration on her television.

The poet Robert Frost is at the podium to recite a poem. He wrote it special for the inauguration. Only he is old, and the sun is so bright reflecting off the snow that he can't see the words to read on the paper in front of him. It reminds me of Mrs. Lazarus. I miss her. Robert Frost decides to recite a different poem, one that he knows by heart. When it is time for John Fitzgerald Kennedy to take the oath of office and deliver his speech, he does it without the silk top hat and overcoat he was wearing in the Capitol building. I see his bubble of breath as he speaks. If he's freezing, nobody can tell. His speech is not very long. He said some things that made me feel like he was talking right to me. He said something about making God's work on earth our own. That sounded exactly like what Rabbi Levine always tells us. That everybody has to do their part to repair all of the holes in the world.

Sy leaves at around two in the afternoon so Auntie Rina can rest. He promises to be back tomorrow. I know he will be. I can tell that Sy is one to keep his promises. Mummy is going to make a nice dinner for everyone. We're having veal and peppers with spaghetti. Lots of things have changed around here, including the dinner menus. Finally! Mummy makes new dishes all the time now. And we're going to eat in the downstairs dining room. Mummy says she doesn't believe anymore in saving things for best. Every day should be a special occasion. Uncle Max, Aunt Dolores, and baby Leonard will be joining us for dinner, too. My only first cousin was born on December 13, 1960. Leonard was named after *Bubbie* Lena. He's not a Christmas baby like Aunt

Dolores, which means he's going to be one spoiled kid. He's going to have a birthday, Christmas, and Hanukkah all in the same month.

Once Sy leaves, it's time for me and Marty to break one old promise and to keep a new one. We dress once again for the weather and go out to the garage. I take my snow shovel and Marty pushes the snowblower. As we walk down the middle of Darlene Avenue I think about Robert Frost standing at that inaugural podium. In English class we discussed his poem "Stopping by Woods on a Snowy Evening." Some kids thought it was just about going on a journey on horseback through the woods, and other kids thought it was about dying. Maybe it's about both. Maybe it's about something very simple and also about something more complicated. Maybe that's what everything in life is about, anyway.

"'The woods are lovely, dark and deep, but I have promises to keep,'" I say out loud.

"Hey, I know that one," Marty says. "Seventh-grade English. 'And miles to go before I sleep.'"

We stand on Darlene Avenue right in front of the big white Victorian. The driveway is two feet deep in snow. Only the wraparound porch looks swept. Even the best brooms in the world couldn't clean this heavy snow off the driveway.

"You know, Marty," I say to my brother. "I think being the president of the United States is a lot like being the Lone Ranger."

"Oh yuh?"

"Well, think of the Lone Ranger's creed. 'I believe...that all men are created equal and that everyone has within himself the power to make this a better world,'" I say.

"And 'that sooner or later, somewhere, somehow, we must settle with the world and make payment for what we have taken,'" Marty quotes.

"That applies to us, too," I say.

"I know," Marty agrees. "A fiery horse with the speed of light, a cloud of dust—"

"'And a hearty "Hi-yo, Silver, away!"'" I finish.

I shovel a single path up to the front door while Marty pushes the snowblower up and down their driveway. I will go in first, and Marty will join me once he's done with his job. I plant my shovel in some snow by the wraparound porch and kick my boots together to clean them off.

I ring the doorbell and the two sisters, Bronislawa and Ludmila, open the door. I have never seen them up close like this before. Their old faces are deeply lined and their blue eyes are faded. But they have warm smiles. They nod to me as they reach out in welcome and usher me inside their home. From the hallway I can see into the kitchen. There's something cooking in a big pot on the stove. It smells so good. I think it's chicken soup.

39
Dear Abby

THE WHITE HOUSE
WASHINGTON

February 2, 1961

Dear Miss Abigail Leah Shapiro,
    I received all ten of your letters yesterday, on the first of February. They were bundled with twine according to date and mailed inside a manila envelope to the office of Senator John Fitzgerald Kennedy in Washington, DC. The envelope was postmarked September 2, 1960. I realize that was five months ago. Please understand that the volume of mail that comes my way is enormous, and is often misplaced in the mail room. I believe that is what happened to this manila envelope.
    I was somewhat confused about the circumstances of the letters. There was no note of explanation inside of the envelope. And then there was the mystery of why they'd been mailed by a Miss Bronislawa Syszmanski of 76 Darlene Avenue, and not by a

Miss Abigail Leah Shapiro of 52 Darlene Avenue. So I was left to draw my own conclusions. Please inform me if I am incorrect in my assumptions.

Abby, you wrote to me filled with such genuine enthusiasm for your fashion designs. Every time you burst into a description of the ensembles, I imagined I had a front-row seat at a Paris fashion show watching the latest creations from the House of Abilea Coutures being modeled. You are, indeed, a very talented young lady. Your designs show great promise and a flair for simplicity and quiet elegance. Each design created for me was perfect, reflecting my own sense of style. I loved how you turned simple frocks into something quite special with accessories such as bows or beading.

I do not know why your letters were never originally mailed. Perhaps you opened them and changed your mind. Several of them had little pebbles and pine needles inside the envelopes. That part of the puzzle remains a mystery. But what is quite clear is your sense of frustration. I am so sorry about that. Had I received the letters, I most definitely would have responded. Please believe me that I never would have ignored you.

I also regret not being able to read the letters during those troubled periods in your life. I am deeply honored that you reached out to me for advice and comfort. All families experience trying and difficult moments. However, most problems have solutions. Nothing ever is as important as your family and the love you have for one another. Please, Abby, remember that always.

You and I do, indeed, have much in common. I, too, deplore wearing gloves. I keep them on in public for photographs and then pull them off as quickly as possible. They are so uncomfortable. I also loved to sketch fashion designs as a young girl. I had the habit of rushing through exams so I could sketch new dresses on the back of my test papers. I was often sent to the headmistress's office at boarding school for a scolding. I do love fashion, but it is not the most important thing in my life. I was quite puzzled during President Kennedy's campaign. All the talk over what I wore and how I fixed my hair had nothing to do with my husband's ability to be president. My favorite clothes are comfortable slacks and sweaters. That way I can get on the floor and play with my children.

I have a special dinner date with the president on February 14, Valentine's Day. I plan on wearing that beautiful dress you designed for me last Valentine's Day. And do not fret, I have instructed my seamstress not to change one detail. I will request that the White House photographer take some shots, and I will send them to you. Thank you so much for everything.

Abby, please let me know that you have received this letter and that you are doing well. I don't know if Miss Bronislawa Syszmanski is a personal friend of yours, but I think she deserves a thank-you from both of us. She did us a great service. And finally, I believe, as does the president, that the future of our great country lies with our young people. I know that you are, and will be, a shining example for your generation.

Bye!
Your Friend in Fashion,
  Jacqueline Lee Bouvier Kennedy (But please call
     me Jackie)

P.S. May I have a wallet-size photograph from sixth
grade where you are wearing that purple-and-
sky-blue plaid skirt-and-vest set?

P.P.S. Please extend my regards to your entire
family, with thanks for their support during the
presidential campaign.

P.P.P.S. Please thank your Uncle Morris and Auntie
Rina for sending me such comfortable shoes
from your family's store. I enjoy wearing them
tremendously on my rather large feet! (Don't
worry, Abby, that was just a joke.)

P.P.P.P.S. I was never offended that you wanted to
charge for your designs. You are a professional. I
admired your work ethic in devising a plan to save
for a Barbie doll.

P.P.P.P.P.S. I am so sorry that your experiment with
Barbie was a disaster. However, I am flattered
that you wanted to turn her into me.

P.P.P.P.P.P.S. No, my daughter Caroline does not have a
Barbie doll. I think she is a little too young to play
with a Barbie.

P.P.P.P.P.P.P.S. I do not remember the exact age when

I was fitted for my first bra. But I will confess to being a late bloomer.

P.P.P.P.P.P.P.S. Please let me know if your family ever travels to Washington, DC. I would love to give you a personal tour of the White House.

P.P.P.P.P.P.P.P.S. I am a righty, just like you!

P.P.P.P.P.P.P.P.P.S. I beat you on the P.S.s!

40

Bon Voyage, Headless Barbie

Today is Saturday, March 11, 1961. Six months have passed since my twelfth birthday, but I am just getting around to celebrating it today.

Anna Maria rings my doorbell and we head down Darlene Avenue. We pass the big white Victorian with the wraparound porch. The sisters are already outside sweeping.

"Bronislawa, Ludmila, *dzień dobry*," I shout across the street.

The sisters wave back.

"Can I come by later for a visit?"

The sisters nod yes.

Anna Maria grabs my arm. "Abby, what's the matter, did they cast a spell on you? Were you just speaking witch language?"

"Of course not, silly. I said good morning in Polish. Bronislawa and Ludmila taught me that. They come from Poland and they are my friends."

"WHAT! How did this happen and why didn't you tell me?"'

I take a deep breath and think for a minute about how and what I will tell Anna Maria. Even though she is my best friend, I never told her the whole story. I was too ashamed.

"Well, what happened was that Mummy made a mistake with the outgoing and the incoming mail," I say. "And my letters to

Jackie got lost for a very long time. But don't worry. It had nothing to do with your father and the US mail."

"Oh," Anna Maria says.

Anna Maria is no dummy. She probably gets the picture.

"But then what happened is that Bronislawa found the letters. She saw that they were addressed to Senator John Fitzgerald Kennedy's office, so she stuck them all together in one big envelope and mailed them. They felt it was the patriotic thing to do."

"Patriotic? You mean they're American?" Anna Maria says.

"Of course they're American, just like us."

"Wow," Anna Maria says. "And they're nice?"

"Very nice. Want to meet them later?"

"Sure."

We walk about a mile until we get to Susie's house. She's waiting for us on the front lawn. The three of us continue to D.W. Field Park, where we stop at the waterfall.

"Where do you think the stream ends up?" I say.

"Probably in a river," Susie says.

"Then maybe the ocean," Anna Maria adds. "Who knows?"

"Are you ready for the farewell ceremony?" Susie asks.

"Yuh. Never been readier," I answer.

We put our knapsacks on the ground. I remove Headless Barbie from my knapsack and hold her high above the waterfall.

"*Bon voyage,* Headless Barbie," I say as I let her go.

"*Au revoir,*" Anna Maria says.

"*Oui, oui, bon jour,* Headless Barbie," Susie says.

Anna Maria rolls her eyes but doesn't say anything, because Susie doesn't take French like we do. She signed up for Latin.

The three of us wave good-bye as Headless Barbie is carried downstream. I wonder if she'll be found by another girl somewhere who has a Barbie head without a body. Or maybe she'll wash up on a shore of the Atlantic Ocean somewhere and meet up with Auntie Rina's long-lost rag doll. Who knows? Anything in this life is possible, even being friends with Susie Applegate.

Susie became the leper of seventh grade after her father's arrest and conviction. Kids sang the leprosy song at her when she walked down the hallways in between classes: "Susie's got leprosy, I don't want it crawling all over me. There goes Susie's eyeball, into my highball. There goes Susie's fingernail, into my ginger ale."

Mummy said the only reason I wanted a Barbie was because Susie had one. She was right. I was jealous. But Susie also told me that she was jealous of me and Anna Maria and our special friendship. She said that she wished she could live in my house because there was always something to do or somebody different to talk to if you went upstairs or downstairs. She also complimented me on the Pink Palace and my shelves of dolls. She thought they were so wonderful, they should be in a museum.

Susie takes a blanket out of her knapsack and we spread it out beside the waterfall. This is where we'll have my birthday party. I have cupcakes and my friends have presents for me. Anna Maria's gift is a regular blond Dressed for Swim and Fun Barbie with a ponytail to replace my destroyed doll. Nonna Adelaide sewed a complete wardrobe of my designs and had special tiny labels made for the clothes. They say "Design by Abilea Coutures." Susie's gift is a brunette Barbie with a bubble hairdo.

"Look what the toy company did," Anna Maria says when she sees the brunette Barbie. "They gave her the bubble cut so she'd look just like Jackie. They're copycats, Abby! You had the idea first. You're the one who told Jackie to cut her hair like that. You always have the ideas first."

"Not without your help," I say to Anna Maria.

"True," she agrees. "I did play a big part in all of this."

Anna Maria's pixie has all grown out. She doesn't have bangs anymore, so the only twirling she'll be doing in the future is with her baton.

Turns out that Susie, Anna Maria, and me aren't the only girls in West Junior High who still play with dolls. In February we formed an after-school club, calling it the Dolls Forever Club. Each week we bring one or two of our favorite dolls and tell their stories. Some of the girls are collectors like me and some only play with Barbies. I've shared all of my designs, and some girls are getting extra credit in home economics class making the doll clothes on the sewing machine.

The first doll I shared with the Dolls Forever Club was Mei. She has been back home safe and sound since the day of President Kennedy's inauguration. That was when me and Marty shoveled and plowed Bronislawa and Ludmila's driveway and apologized for what we did to them. The sisters had found Mei in their woods and taken good care of her. They knew all along that it was me who sprayed the shaving cream and pitched the eggs. They were patiently waiting for me to ring their doorbell. They knew someday I would come. And I was right when I told Marty that all they were doing was saving those wiffle balls in the pail for us.

There is a reason why they would never sell their woods to Harry Degen's father. It is because it reminded them of their home in Europe before World War II. When the Nazis invaded Poland, the sisters joined the resistance movement. They smuggled Jewish children to safety through their woods and hid them with Polish families or with priests and nuns in monasteries. But they were caught by the Nazis, who sent them to prison and tortured them. That's why their bodies are so bent and broken. Mr. Lane was right when he called them angels. When I told Auntie Rina all about them and how they saved Jewish children from death in concentration camps, she wept. She said she was so ashamed of herself for assuming terrible things about people she didn't know. Part of her recuperation was to walk every day, so I took her over to meet Bronislawa and Ludmila. They had an extra rocking chair, which they brought out on the porch. Sometimes Auntie Rina sits with them and they talk about the Old Countries.

Susie, Anna Maria, and me are already making plans for the Dolls Forever Club for eighth grade. We've asked for a larger room because this year we had to turn some girls away. And we don't like that. Nobody should be excluded from joining. I'm the president of the club and I made up an oath. It goes like this: I, Abigail Leah Shapiro, (and all the members say their names) love dolls. And if I want to play with dolls until I'm one hundred and ten, then that is my right because this is America, where people have freedom to make choices for themselves.

41
Belka, Strelka, and Nikita

ABIGAIL LEAH SHAPIRO

August 13, 1961

Dear Jackie,
    You are the best pen pal ever! I love
getting your letters in the mail. The one
from last week cracked me up. You are such
a card! I think that is the funniest
story I've heard in a long time. I picture
the whole scene. There you are in June, at
the Schoenbrunn Palace in Vienna, Austria,
with President Kennedy and Nikita
Krushchev. And the leader of the Soviet
Union says, "I'd like to shake her hand
first." I think somebody has a crush on
you! Was President Kennedy jealous? He
shouldn't be. Mr. Krushchev is not nearly
as handsome as the president. Not even
close! Mr. Krushchev is bald and fat, and
President Kennedy has, as Mummy puts it,
"a lush head of hair." And if you ask me, I

think the Soviet guy is a little scary-looking, too.

I think the best part of your story is when you're talking to Mr. Kruschev about the astronaut dogs. I remember hearing about Belka and Strelka last summer on the nightly news. I told Anna Maria how you joked with Mr. Kruschev about giving you one of Strelka's puppies. Who knew that the Soviet ambassador would actually ring the doorbell at the White House with a present for Caroline? I think the name of Caroline's new puppy is perfect, since Pushinka means "fluffy" in Russian, and puppies are fluffy. Anna Maria wants to know if the FBI frisked Pushinka to make sure she wasn't a spy. Oh, that just reminded me of Mad magazine. Marty gets it now in the mail instead of Popular Mechanics. They've got this cartoon strip in there called "Spy vs Spy." He says it's really all about the United States and the Soviet Union and this Cold War we're fighting. Anna Maria said that her cousins Rosemary and Rocco had a bomb shelter built in their house.

I have been working like crazy with Rabbi Levine to make sure it's "mission control, three, two, one, zero...liftoff!" for my Bat Mitvah, which is exactly thirteen days from now. I am sorry that you and President Kennedy won't be able to attend. I understand that running the country takes up a lot of time. Rabbi Levine told me that a girl is technically a Bat Mitzvah when she's twelve and one day, and that you don't have to have a ceremony in the synagogue. But having a real Bat Mitzvah is something I've wanted for a very long time. Mummy did a complete about-face in her thinking. "Just because it didn't exist in my day is no reason for you not to have a Bat Mitzvah. Go for it, Abby!" she said. I got a late start on account of Auntie Rina being sick. My family appreciates how you always ask about her health.

Bye!
Your Friend,
Abby

P.S. Thank you for sending me a photograph of the gorgeous, pink shimmery gown you wore in Vienna when Mr. Krushchev flirted with you. You looked so beautiful. I am honored, Jackie, really and truly, that you told your designer, the world famous Mr. Oleg Cassini, to create a gown which was a blend between the one I designed for Auntie Rina (if she was going to the inauguration) and the inaugural gown for you with the shimmery bodice.

P.P.S. Big News! Abilea Coutures had a very special commission-Auntie Rina's wedding dress! Next Sunday she will marry Sy at my Uncle Max's nightclub, the Pink Elephant. Rabbi Levine says this will be the first time he's ever married a couple in a nightclub. Sy is Auntie Rina's meant-to-be husband, only she didn't know it for more than forty years. But Sy always knew it, so he waited. How do you like that? That's some love story! Auntie Rina said at her age she didn't want a regular bride's gown, just a nice, pretty party dress. Here's a copy of the sketch. What do you think? Anna Maria's Nonna Adelaide sewed the dress as a wedding gift for Auntie Rina. My inspiration came from the dress on my doll from Mexico.

P.P.P.S. Speaking of pictures, here's a photograph of my doll Mei back home safe and sound. I forgot to tell you that the two sisters, Bronislawa Syszmanski and her sister, Ludmila, found Mei in their woods back on Halloween 1959.

P.P.P.P.S. If you do get a chance to look at any issues of Mad, check out the one from March. It was a really neat issue. It was the "upside-up" issue. Write 1961 on a piece of paper. Then turn it around. Get it?

P.P.P.P.P.S. Anna Maria asked me to ask you a favor. If it's possible, could you get an autograph from Alan Shepard? He's her hero.

We watched the whole Mercury Freedom 7 liftoff from Cape Canaveral on television, and Anna Maria has decided that she wants to be an astronaut when she grows up. She figures that if the two female dogs made it to space and back, so can real ladies. So Anna Maria wants to be ready when President Kennedy wins the space race and sends people to the moon.

42

Today I Am a Woman And in Two Weeks I'll Be a Teenager

The sounds of "Let's twist again, like we did last summer" fill the social hall of the synagogue. The forty-fives are stacked high on the record player, and drop as each song ends. Tonight Uncle Morris is the official disc jockey for my Bat Mitzvah party. I teased him and said he was a regular Dick Clark. "Yowzah!" he said. I know he didn't have a clue who I was talking about, but I think he's doing a pretty good job for someone who's not used to rock and roll music.

"Marty, nice moves," I whisper to my brother as I work the crowd. Weeks of after-school dance practice have paid off. He's twisting like crazy with his date, Marcy. She's in his high school history class. I can tell she likes Marty because when she twists, she leans in really close.

There are so many people here. My family, neighbors, Marty's friends, my friends from the Dolls Forever Club, and, of course, some boys from my classes. After all, the girls need dance partners.

"Here, Abby," Aunt Dolores says, handing me baby Lenny. "He wants to dance with you."

I kick off my black patent leather pumps and pick up my baby cousin, which is not so easy. He's one cute little butterball. I can't believe he's nearly a year old. Auntie Rina sure is right when she says time flies. Lenny laughs and drools on my cheek as I twist with him and sing the words to the Chubby Checker song. His pudgy fingers touch the strand of pearls around my neck.

"Play nice, Lenny," I tell him. "Don't tug, okay?"

The strand of pearls with matching earrings were Mummy's Bat Mitzvah gift to me. The necklace is very beautiful and has a white-gold clasp with little diamond chips. They must have cost a fortune. Mummy said that every fashionable woman should have a strand of pearls in her jewelry box because they go with everything, from party dresses to sweaters and pants. When I opened the earring box, I said, "But, Mummy, these are for pierced ears. I don't have pierced ears."

"Well then, we'll have to do something about that, won't we?" she said.

That afternoon, which was two days before my Bat Mitzvah, Mummy took me to Dr. Korim's office and he marked spots on my earlobes with a blue ballpoint pen. For a second I got very nervous. It reminded me of the Barbie-Jackie disaster.

"I hope that pen doesn't leak," I said.

"Of course not. I always get a bull's-eye."

Dr. Korim stuck a needle straight through each of the marked earlobes, swabbed them with alcohol, and placed my new pearl earrings right through the holes. "There you go, young lady, you're all set."

Auntie Rina's gift to me was a complete surprise. When we arrived in synagogue on Friday evening before services, I saw our family's silver candlesticks from the Old Country set out on a small table with a white cloth in the sanctuary.

"They belong to you now, just like I promised," Auntie Rina said.

"I will light candles on the Sabbath and for the holidays," I told Auntie Rina. "That's part of being a Bat Mitzvah and carrying out the commandments. But, I am not going to follow any of your cockamamy, superstitious traditions from the Old Country."

"*Oy, keynehore,* poo poo poo! Don't say that! Not even one?"

"Okay, maybe just one," I said.

"Or two?"

"Don't push it, Auntie Rina."

When Rabbi Levine motioned to me that it was time to light the candles to usher in the Sabbath, I whispered to Auntie Rina that I'd like to have Mummy say the blessing with me. She smiled and said, "That's my girl." Me and Mummy have been down a long road, but we're working on our relationship step-by-step, filling up those holes in our lives one by one.

Susie Applegate is singing along to Ricky Nelson: "I'm a travelin' man, I've made a lot of stops all over the world..." She's singing a little too loud because she's drowning out the forty-five. Anna Maria goes over to her and they giggle. Then they both run over me to.

"This party is a blast," Anna Maria says.

"Yuh, a real gas," Susie says.

"Somebody's got a girlfriend," Anna Maria says, pointing to Marty slow dancing with Marcy.

"Betcha there'll be some germ warfare later on," Susie says.

Me and Anna Maria look at each other and mouth, "Eew!"

"Jinx, double jinx, infinity jinx," Anna Maria says, punching me in the arm.

"Ya know, Abby, I just thought of something cool," Susie says.

"What?"

"Today you are a woman, but in two weeks you're going to be thirteen. That means you'll be both a woman and a teenager at the same time."

"Cool," Anna Maria says.

I nod and smile. I like that. I like it a lot.

"Uh, Abby, you wanna dance?" asks Todd Silver.

Marty has been back being friends with Todd Silver and Harry Degen for a while. Mummy said she didn't mind as long as they kept their noses clean and didn't do stupid and dangerous things like light hydrogen bubbles anymore.

"Wait until the song changes," I say. "I want to fast dance."

The record player drops another forty-five and the saxophone starts wailing to "Quarter to Three." I grab Todd's hand and drag him to the center of the dance floor. I think this teenager business is going to work out great!

43
Bread and Butter

ABIGAIL LEAH SHAPIRO

November 11, 1961

Dear Jackie,

   Many thanks to you and President
Kennedy for the generous gifts. The US
savings bond is already tucked away in the
bank safety-deposit box, where it will
grow interest for my college fund. Mummy
says that college is practically around
the corner. Well, it is for Marty, anyway.
Did I tell you that I am taking typing
this year? Marty told me to do it because
it will make writing papers a lot easier.

   I don't know how you knew it, but I did
not have a doll from Peru in my collection.
I love her! She's very happy on her spot on
the top glass shelf getting to know her
new friends. You know, since you're the
First Lady and get to meet world leaders,
why not start Caroline on a foreign doll

collection? I know she'll thank you for it when she gets a little bit older. Speaking of Caroline and world leaders, how is Pushinka? Is she White Housebroken??

My Bat Mitzvah weekend went off without a hitch. I led the service Friday night, and on Saturday morning when I read from the Torah. Rabbi Levine hugged me when I finished and congratulated me for an "exemplary" job. I was sweating it that I'd make a mistake, but I didn't flub any Hebrew words. Saturday night after sundown we celebrated with a big party in my honor. But becoming a Bat Mitzvah is more than fun and games. There's a lot of responsibility that goes with it. Rabbi Levine said that it's not only about following the Jewish commandments but also about finding meaning in my life and doing my bit to make the world a better place. Rabbi Levine's been drilling that message since I started Hebrew school, and it really sunk in. I told him he sounded like President Kennedy and he said, "Thanks for the compliment." Anyway, I'm up to the challenge. So here comes Abigail Leah Shapiro!!

Jackie, my Bat Mitzvah dresses were fab! I was inspired by everything Auntie Rina showed me in the magazines about this new fashion scene that's all over London, England. Hemlines are up, dresses have high waistlines with skirts flaring out like a capital A, and they say in a few years,

the colors will be wild. Nonna Adelaide
really wanted to make them for me, but the
arthritis in her fingers flared up after
doing the trim on Auntie Rina's wedding
dress. So Mummy suggested that we take on
the challenge as a mother-daughter project.
I said, "Mummy, I didn't know you could
sew." And she said, "There are a lot of things
you don't know about me." The project was a
success—both the dresses and us working as
a team. I'm sending you the sketches of my
dresses for old time's sake.

   Love,
   Abby (Your friend in fashion and in a
      whole lot more)

P.S. Please say hello to the president and
to Caroline, and give little John-John a
hug. He's got a first birthday coming up
just like my baby cousin, Lenny. Maybe
someday they can meet and play. Maybe if
my whole family visits Washington, DC,
during cherry blossom time, I'll take you
up on that offer to give us a personal tour
of the White House.

P.P.S Eighth grade so far is great. The
members of the Dolls Forever Club are
having a bake sale this week to raise
money to buy Thanksgiving groceries
for needy families. I also get a ton of
homework, so please understand if I don't

write as often as I did in the past. It doesn't mean I'm not thinking about you. It's just means that I'm busy.

P.P.P.S. Wait one sec, Jackie, Mummy's knocking on the Pink Palace's door.

P.P.P.P.S. I'm back! Mummy came in to show me a note she got from a neighbor, Mrs. Whelan. She's the lady across the street who's had lots of troubles and once had a run-in with Mummy. But that was a long time ago when things were different. Mummy said Mrs. Whelan wrote a very gracious bread-and-butter note, thanking her for the invitation to my Bat Mitzvah and also for always lending a helping hand when she was down and out. I said, "That was very nice of Mrs. Whelan, but why in the world is it called a bread-and-butter note?" Mummy said, and I think I'll quote her, because it might have been one of the smartest things that ever came out of her mouth.

"They're called bread-and-butter notes because bread and butter are the basics, the staff of life. They taste great and keep you alive if you have nothing else to eat. You can always count on bread and butter. And having good manners, saying thank you for someone's kindness or generosity is also a basic of life. It makes you feel good to write the note and it sustains the person who's receiving the note."

Mummy's answer really got me thinking. So I want to thank you one more time, not just for the Bat Mitzvah gifts, but for everything else. Mrs. Jacqueline Lee Bouvier Kennedy, First Lady of the United States of America, thank you for being my bread and butter. Get my drift?

Friday Night Outfit

black velvet headband

No more ponytail
New hairstyle
"the bob"

pearl earrings

Pink frosted lipstick

pearl necklace

Cutaway black velvet jacket

3/4" sleeve with lace trim

black patent leather belt

beige linen sleeveless dress
(Jackie, I really wanted this dress to be hot pink, but Mummy said not appropriate for synagogue)

lace trim goes all the way up to the right shoulder

silk stockings

Abibea Couture

black patent leather pumps

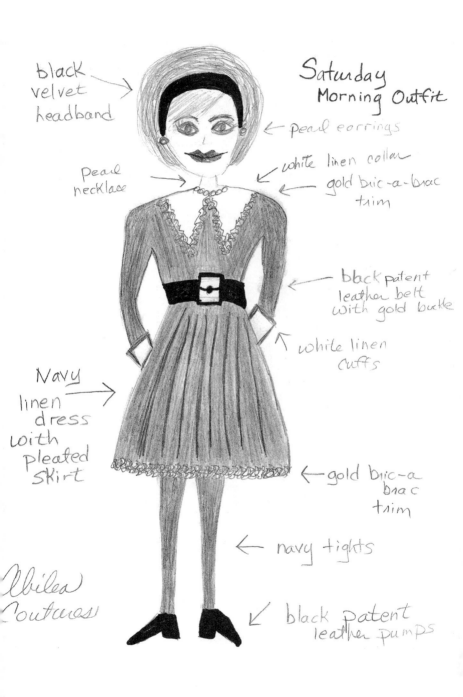

black velvet headband

Saturday Morning Outfit

← pearl earrings

white linen collar

gold bric-a-brac trim

Pearl necklace

black patent leather belt with gold buckle

white linen cuffs

Navy linen dress with pleated skirt

gold bric-a brac trim

← navy tights

black patent leather pumps

Abilea Coutures

Black silk headscarf

Saturday Night Party Dress

Pink frosted lipstick and eye makeup

Mummy said "yes" to HOT PINK and to a short hemline!!

black

white

Hot pink

Jersey Knit Dress

Hot pink and black checks

black tights

black patent leather pumps

Abilea Coutures

Glossary and Pronunciation of Yiddish and Hebrew Words

Pronunciation Key:

kh: has a "clearing your throat" sound, as in the Scottish word "loch"

tsh: has a ch sound, as in children

A klog iz mir! (**A klawg** iz meer) Woe is me!

baleboste (bah-leh-**boss**-teh) A terrific homemaker

Bar Mitzvah (bahr-**mitz**-vah) A ceremony in the synagogue for Jewish boys at the age of thirteen. The words "Bar Mitzvah" come from Hebrew and literally mean "son of the commandment." When a boy becomes a Bar Mitzvah, he is considered a man by his synagogue community and able to fulfill his religious responsibilities.

Bat Mitzvah (baht-**mitz**-vah) A ceremony in the synagogue for Jewish girls any time after the age of twelve. The words "Bat Mitzvah" come from Hebrew and literally mean "daughter of the commandment." When a girl becomes a Bat Mitzvah, she is considered a woman by her synagogue community and is able to fulfill her religious responsibilities.

bashert (bah-**share**-t) Something that is destined, fated, meant-to-be

Bubbie (buh-bee) Grandmother

bupkes (bup-kess) An angry word, meaning you got nothing after a lot of work or effort. It literally means "beans."

chametz (khah-mets) Leavened bread, not to be eaten at Passover

charpe (khahr-peh) A disgrace

chutzpa (khoots-pah) Nerve, gall

dreidel (dray-dell) A four-sided top with Hebrew letters played with during the holiday of Hanukkah

farshteyst (far-**shtay**-st) Understand?

farshtopte (far-**shtop**-teh) Stuffed up, as in *farshtopte kop* (stuffed-up head, forgetful)

farshtunkene (far-**shtoonk**-en-eh) Stinking

feh (feh) Exclamation of disgust

gelt (gelt) Money

genug (geh-**noog)** Enough! End of conversation!

hak mir nisht ken tshaynik (hahk mir nisht ken **cheye**-nick) Literal translation is "stop knocking on my teapot." Stop talking, stop driving me crazy.

Hanukkah (hah-noo-kah) An eight-day Jewish festival usually occurring in December. Candles are lit every night in the menorah. The holiday commemorates the rededication of the temple in Jerusalem.

keynehore (kay-neh-**haw**-reh) This is a contraction of words that means *no evil eye*! Often followed by *poo poo poo*!

kop (kawp) A head

kosher (ko-share or **ko**-sher) Foods prepared according to Jewish dietary laws

kvetch (kvetch rhymes with fetch) To complain

machsheyfe (makh-**shay**-feh) A witch

matzoh (maht-sa) Unleavened bread eaten during Passover

maven (may-ven) An expert, an authority

mazel tov (mah-zell **toe-v)** Congratulations! Literal translation from Hebrew is "good luck."

meshugge (meh-**shoog**-gah) Crazy

meshuggener (meh-**shoog**-gen-er) A crazy person

mitzvah (**mitz**-vah) A good deed

narishkayt (**nahr**-ish-kite) Foolishness

noch a mol (**nawkh**-a-mal) One more time

noch a mayse (**nawkh** a **my**-seh) Yet another story

nudnik (**nood**-nick) An annoying bore

oyverbotl (**oyver**-bawtl) Senile, confused

pupik (**poo**-pick) Belly button

Rosh Hashanah (rawsh-ha-**shah**-nah) A two-day holiday
    marking the Jewish New Year

shande (**shahn**-deh) A shame

sheyne ponim (**shay**-ney **paw**-nim) A pretty face

shikker (**shick**-ker) A drunk

shiksa (**shick**-sah) A non-Jewish woman

shiva (**shi**-vah) A seven-day period of mourning after the
    death of a family member

shlep (**shlep**) To drag

shmatte (**shmah**-teh) A rag

shmooze (**shmooz**) Friendly chitchat

shpilkes (**shpill**-kess) Restless, sitting on pins and needles

shvester (**shvest**-er) Sister

Torah (**Toe**-rah) The Jewish Bible, the Five Books of Moses

treyf (**trayf**) Food that is not kosher

tsuris (**tsoo**-riss) Troubles, worries

tsvey (**tsvay**) Two

tush (**tush** rhymes with push) Bottom, behind, derriere

vos vilstu (vawss-**vill**-stoo) What do you want?

yenta (**yen**-tah) A gossip, a troublemaker

Yiddish (**yid**-dish) The language spoken by Jews in eastern
    Europe

Yom Kippur (yom-**key**-poor) The Jewish Day of Repentance.
    It is a day of fasting.

Author's Note

Although *Your Friend in Fashion* is a work of fiction, there are a number of similarities between Abby's childhood and mine. I am a doll collector, and like Abby, believe that you never get too old to play with dolls. I owned one of the original Barbie dolls with the black-and-white-striped bathing suit until the day I decided to make her over into Jackie Kennedy. The "experiment" as described in the book is true. I also wanted to be Jackie Kennedy's personal fashion designer and sketched glamorous clothes for her to wear. All of the fashion designs in the book are original, dating from 1959–1962. The last three designs were created in 2010 for this story.

Acknowledgments

Thanks to my readers: David Axelrod, Michael Axelrod, Ann Bauch, Jessica Benach, and Leslie Taubman Friedman.

And another big thanks to my agent, Nancy Gallt, and to my editor, Julie Amper.

To find out more about Amy Axelrod, visit her website: www.amyaxelrod.com.